THE TRUTH
ABOUT
STONE HOLLOW

•

THE TRUTH ABOUT STONE HOLLOW

Zilpha Keatley Snyder

Illustrated by Alton Raible

A YEARLING BOOK

to Jean

THE TRUTH
ABOUT
STONE HOLLOW

chapter one

Strangers sometimes called them mountains, but to Taylor Valley people they were always just the Hills. They rose in ranks on each side of the valley floor, from low, rolling foothills, up and up to the farthest crest, steep and jagged, and dark against the thin blue air. Wooded, rocky, and crevassed by canyons, they shut the valley off from highways and railroads, and many other things which, by the year 1938, were not so very far away.

In that year, a narrow potholed strip of warped blacktop known as the Old Road was still the only way to get to the Hunter farm from the town of Taylor Springs, and it was along that road that Amy walked, or more often ran, on her way to school.

One Monday in late September, Amy trotted

around the corner of the schoolhouse and right into a clump of children who were watching Gordie Parks shove someone against the schoolhouse wall. Above the heads of smaller children, Amy could see Gordie's face, wild and red with bully-anger. Eyes set and bulgy and cheeks jiggling, Gordie was slamming a new boy against the wall again and again.

From the edge of the crowd, Amy pushed past Alice Harris and Shirley Anderson, ducked around Jed Lewis, and stopped where she could get a good look at the new boy, who was almost hidden by the bulk of Gordie. He was ugly, she decided, as stringy and scrawny as a half-grown chicken. His face, as white as Gordie's was red, was winced into a grimace that stretched his lips into pale ribbons and hid his eyes in tight, drawn wrinkles. But he would have been strange-looking even if he hadn't been making a face.

For one thing, his clothes were wrong—a Sunday kind of suit, tweedy and short-legged, instead of real school clothes, and old-fashioned shoes, high and shiny. His hair was thick and shaggy and of the streaky blond color that turns greenish when it needs a washing. But the difference about him was more than you could point to—more strange and foreign-looking than things like clothes, shoes, and haircuts could explain.

As Amy inched closer, Gordie slammed the boy again, so hard that his head bounced on the school

4

wall, and his teeth snapped together like a beetle-clicker. Amy's hand twitched toward the back of her own head, and she caught her breath as her stomach tightened with excitement. She moved up again, into the front row of the crowd.

Gordie looked around then and, encouraged by the size of his audience, he forced out more and fiercer fury. "You stinking sissy," he growled. "Why don't you fight, you Goddamned stinking sissy?" Balling up his fat fist he swung it hard, right at the new boy's mouth.

The boy jolted backward and then stood still with his hands covering his face. When he let them drop, the grimace was gone. His face had gone limp and quiet. There was blood on his lip and his eyes were wide and white-rimmed like the eyes of a frightened horse. When they turned toward Amy, she saw that they were blue and bewildered-looking, and suddenly the greedy excitement in her stomach curdled into a sick feeling and she shrank backward through the crowd. Once she was safely outside the circle, she ran.

She dashed across the school grounds and pounded with forbidden speed down the hallway to the door of Room 6. Flinging it open, she burst into words before there was time to remember about Miss McMillan and tattling.

Miss McMillan, who was so tiny and weak that sixth-grade boys had to open jar lids and lift boxes for her, believed in being strong. She believed in strength and individualism and "standing on your own two feet," and in her classroom tattlers often found themselves in more trouble than the people who got tattled on. Her frown reminded Amy before she was good and started, but by then it was too late to stop.

"—and Gordie socked him in the mouth and his lip's bleeding and he's way littler, Miss McMillan, and skinny, too."

Miss McMillan's frown had changed to a mocking smile. "Well, Amy. Tattling already? So early on a Monday morning?"

"But Miss McMillan, his lip—"

"Amy, my dear. Calm down. This is just something that has been going on since boys were first invented, and will keep on happening as long as boys are boys. It's best, you'll find, to let them work it out between—"

"But Miss McMillan," Amy interrupted desperately, "Gordie is swearing. He said Goddamn right out loud—in front of first-graders, too."

Miss McMillan's mocking smile faded, and she stood up. Straightening her skirt with a jerk, she headed for the door. Amy followed at a safe distance until they reached the corner, and then she turned and ran the other way. She hid out in the girls' rest room and stayed there until the bell rang, and then came out pretending not to know what all the excitement was about.

Surprisingly, it worked. Nobody found out that Amy had been the one who tattled. The fight watchers had been so hypnotized by Gordie's raging that they had not noticed when Amy turned and ran. And for once Miss McMillan did not mention the tattling, shaming the tattler and urging everyone to fight his own battles and stand on his own two feet. Amy couldn't guess why she'd been so lucky—unless Miss McMillan had finally noticed that some people's feet were bigger and stronger than others and that Amy would have needed a lot more help than her two feet if Gordie found out she was the one who had told on him. But, for whatever lucky reason, nobody seemed to know what she had done. It wasn't until after school that she found out that someone else did know—and that someone was the new boy himself.

His name was Jason Ulysses Fitzmaurice, and he came running out at Amy from behind a clump of eucalyptus trees on the way home from school that afternoon. She heard a voice call, "Look!" and then there he was running toward her, looking down into his cupped hands so intently that he tumbled over the rough ground as if he were running in the dark. He staggered to a stop and, still looking down into his hands, he said, "Look. Look what I found," in a strange, breathless voice.

Amy felt uneasy. If she had not already heard people saying so, she would have guessed right at that moment that he was crazy. "Mad as a March Hare,"

Aunt Abigail would have said. It was mad to run up to a person you didn't know at all and start to talk to them as if you'd known them all your life—especially if that person had seen you beaten and shamed that very morning before half the people in the Taylor Springs School.

"Look," the mad boy said again, "it's alive." His eyes were huge and strangely far apart, like the eyes of an animal. They gleamed up at her, dark blue and shiny, through the curling strands of greenish hair. His nose was short and smallish, his cheeks dented under his eyes instead of bulging, and his upper lip was fat and cracked from Gordie's fist. But even with the fat lip, he didn't look ugly, now that he wasn't making faces. Not ugly, but certainly strange and outlandish—like a person from a different country, or from an old-timey oil painting.

Keeping her distance, Amy leaned over and peered between the boy's thin fingers. It was only a baby bird.

"It's only a baby bird," she said. "Some kind of swallow, most likely. You'd best put it back in its nest or it will die."

"Die?" the boy said. "Will it really?"

The word "really" went up at the end in a foreign-sounding way, and the boy's excited smile faded into a worried frown. More like a three-year-old than a sixth-grade boy, Amy thought.

"Don't you think I could raise it, if I fed it and kept it very warm?" the boy said.

Gingerly, Amy pulled his fingers apart enough to reveal the little head and beak. "See," she said. "It's an insect eater. You can tell by the beak. It would be easier if it were a seed eater. It's hard to find enough insects. They usually die, 'specially when they're that young. It's better to put them back in the nest if you can find it."

"I'll find it," the boy said, and he glanced around as if he expected to see the nest sitting there on the ground near his feet. Then turning back to Amy he asked hopefully, "Do you know where it is?"

Speaking slowly and distinctly as one might to a first-grader, Amy explained that since the bird was too young to fly, or even to hop, the nest was sure to be very close to where he had found the bird.

Beyond the clump of eucalyptus there was a lone tall sycamore. The boy led the way to a spot not far from its trunk, and Amy showed him what to do next. She showed him how, if the baby bird were put back on the ground and watched from a distance, its calling would bring the parent birds. And by watching the coming and going of the parents, it was sometimes possible to find the place where they had hidden their nest.

Hiding behind a large rock, they watched the parent birds come, just as Amy had said they would, but when the nest was spotted at last, it was in a bad place, far out at the end of a long limber branch.

"Too bad," Amy said. "There's no way to climb

clear up there—no way at all."

But the boy was already sitting on the ground taking off his strange-looking, high-topped shoes. His coat came off next, and he buttoned the little bird into the pocket of his shirt. It took a boost from Amy to get him started up the tall trunk to the first limb, but from there he was on his own.

He was not a good tree climber—not strong and surefooted like Bert Miller, or even delicately balanced like Shirley Anderson, but he was limber and clingy as a monkey, and frighteningly daring. Watching him teeter and dangle, Amy caught her breath a dozen times, and at least three times she yelled at him to give up and come down before he got himself killed. But he kept right on climbing, and at last he reached the nest and got the baby bird into it, and then slithered slowly backward like a strange awkward lizard, until he reached the ground.

Back in the watching spot behind the rock, Amy was still shaky from only watching, but the boy, with blood oozing from the twig scratches on his face and arms, seemed to have forgotten the climb entirely. He peered intently up at the nest, not even noticing Amy's curious stare.

"Do you think they'll accept him?" he asked. "I've read that some birds will reject their own offspring if they've been handled by humans. Do you think they'll reject him?"

"I don't know," Amy said. "Sometimes they won't

have a baby somebody's touched, and sometimes they will. I don't know what they'll do."

The mother bird returned then, and after a few moments she settled contentedly back on the nest, but the boy went on watching her tensely for several minutes longer. When he finally relaxed and stopped bird-watching, Amy was forced to stop watching him. She had been staring, up until then, trying to decide if he was all-the-way crazy, or maybe only a little. It wasn't easy to tell. She'd heard about lots of crazy people and even had known a couple, but they had been grown-ups—an old lady in San Francisco and Grandpa Simmons in Taylor Springs. She had never met a crazy boy before. Some of the "mad as a March Hare" people who figured in Aunt Abigail's stories were dangerous, but the new boy had, so far, done nothing that seemed in any way threatening.

But just at that moment he turned to Amy and, smiling his strange, eager smile, he said, "Thank you for notifying the teacher this morning when I was getting beaten."

Amy was so surprised that she stammered, "How did you—what makes you think—who told you I did it?"

"Nobody told me. I saw you decide to go."

Something tingled at the back of Amy's neck, and she gathered herself together to be ready to leave quickly if it seemed necessary, but there was nothing fiendish or sinister in the boy's smile.

"I don't know what would have happened," the boy said, "if you hadn't called the teacher." He ran his finger carefully over his split and swollen lip.

"That stupid Gordie," Amy said. "He's always fighting. But you should have hit him back. He usually quits if the person fights back."

"I couldn't," the boy said. "I was too frightened."

Amy stared in amazement. For a moment she was too embarrassed to think of anything to say. She'd heard boys admit easily, even proudly, to all sorts of things—things like being dumb or mean or bad but, in Taylor Springs in 1938, boys never admitted to being afraid, not even when they very plainly were. At last she decided the Christian thing to do would be to say something comforting.

"But you weren't afraid in the tree," she said. "You could have been hurt a lot worse in the tree than Gordie could have hurt you."

"Being hurt wasn't what I was afraid of," the boy said.

Feeling uncomfortably like a character from a dream where nothing that happens makes any sense, Amy decided to change the subject.

"Where do you live?" she asked.

"In the brown house at the end of Bradley Lane."

She remembered, then, overhearing people talking at church just the day before, about some city folks who had rented the old Bradley house.

"Where'd you come from?" she asked.

"Do you mean originally," the boy asked, "or most recently?"

Amy looked at him sharply, wondering if he were being smarty—with his big words and funny foreign way of talking. Maybe he thought she didn't know what "originally" meant, or "recently." She knew all right, but she knew something else he probably didn't. She knew it was better to talk like the other kids talked, in Taylor Springs.

"Last!" she said, firmly. "I mean, where did you come from last before here."

"Well, from Berkeley last," he said. "But previously we lived in Athens—that's in Greece—and before that in Barcelona. But I was born in England."

Amy shook her head in amazement. She had known liars before, but not with such good imaginations. She wondered if this Jason had been to any of those places—even one. He lied so convincingly, without any trace of guilty hesitation, that she could almost have believed him, except that no one lived all over the world that way. No one except, perhaps, very rich people. And what would very rich people be doing living in an old worn-out house in Taylor Springs?

"Where do you live, then?" Jason asked.

"Huh?" With an effort Amy brought herself back from wondering about such skillful lying, and realized that she had been asked a question.

"Down that way," she said, pointing, "on the Hunter farm—the big white house with all the porches

14

and the row of pepper trees out front. Mrs. Hunter is my aunt."

"Why do you live with your aunt?" he asked. "Are your parents dead?"

Again the strangeness—as if he didn't realize that "dead" was not a word you used about your own people. People in books or in faraway places could "die" and "be dead" but friends and relatives "passed away" or "crossed over" or even "went to their just reward."

Amy made what she thought of as an Aunt Abigail mouth—a thing that you did with your lips that would make it plain, even to a foreigner, that they had made a foolish mistake. "No," she said. "My parents are not—my parents are alive. They live at my aunt's house, too. We used to live in San Francisco 'til my father broke his back and couldn't work anymore. Then we came back to live in Taylor Springs."

"Came back? You had lived here before, then?"

"No. I hadn't. My mother was born here though. You know the big church right downtown? The Fairchild Community Church? My grandfather was the minister there for thirty-seven years. His name was Reverend Jeremiah Fairchild, and the church is named after him."

"Is that your name—Fairchild?"

"Not my last name. My last name is Polonski. But Fairchild is one of my middle names." Even as she explained about her name, Amy didn't know why she bothered. It was obvious that this new boy didn't know enough about Taylor Springs to know that it was important to have a name like Fairchild. If he stayed very long, though, he would certainly find out.

Suddenly Amy jumped to her feet and dusted off her skirt. "I have to go now," she said. "I promised my aunt I'd hurry home and help her hoe tomatoes."

Jason jumped up, too. "Don't go," he said. "I want to show you something."

"What?"

"A place. A place I found. It's up that way—in the Hills."

Amy guessed almost at once, from the direction the boy was pointing, but she asked anyway. "What kind of place? Is it like a little deep valley on the other side of the first ridge, with an old shack in it?"

"Yes," Jason said. "Like a hidden valley with an old deserted cottage with no windows or doors and some old broken furniture in it and an iron—"

"Furniture?" Amy interrupted. "You didn't go in it, did you?"

"Yes, I went in. I didn't think anyone would mind. There wasn't a door, and it was quite obvious that no one had been there for a long time."

"I'll say no one's been there. No one ever goes there because it's haunted. That's Stone Hollow, and everyone around here knows it's haunted. Did you really go down there? Clear into the house and everything?"

He nodded.

"All by yourself?" Amy asked. When he nodded again, she said, "Gosh! What's it like? What happened? I've been almost there—to where the road starts going down into the hollow. Alice Harris and I went there one time, but we saw something under the big tree near the house, and we got out of there as fast as we could."

"What did you see?"

"I'm not sure," Amy said. "But it was something—" She paused to think. The slight shivery movement that had flickered in the deep shade of the oak trees had grown a little each time she had told about it, and now she let it grow a little more. Letting stories grow a little bit past the absolute truth had been a temptation for as long as she could remember.

"It was something kind of whitish," she said, "with long floppy skinny arms, and eyes like dark holes, like in a skull, and it was swaying back and forth. But what did *you* see? What happened when you went in the house?"

"It was just an old cabin, like a woodcutter's hut. There was a wet moldy smell from all the rain that's leaked in. There are three little rooms, two in front and a long narrow one across the back with a broken table and a rusted iron stove."

"But didn't you see anything scary? Didn't anything happen?"

"No," Jason said, but he looked uncertain. "Nothing actually happened. Not that you can explain about. But I felt—something. There's a difference you can feel right away. That's why I thought you might like to go there—"

"I told you," Amy said, "it's haunted, and nobody goes there. Not even people who don't believe in places being haunted. Nobody I know has been there. Not even people who aren't afraid of anything, like Gordie Parks."

Weirdly, for no reason, Jason began to laugh, and Amy backed away in case he was getting ready to do something even crazier.

"What are you laughing about?" she demanded.

He stopped, then, and after a moment he said, "I was just laughing at what you said—about Gordie. I thought maybe it was a joke."

Amy backed farther. "I have to go now," she said. "I promised my aunt I'd hurry right home from school."

She walked quickly, looking back now and then over her shoulder until the crazy boy was out of sight, and then she began to run.

chapter two

On that day Amy ran all the way home because she was late, but on other days she ran for other reasons. It wasn't just that she liked to run, because she really didn't. There were always other reasons. Just a few days before, she had tried to explain it to her mother.

Shaking her head and sighing as she bandaged Amy's bloody knee, Helen Polonski had asked, "Why were you running? Why do you always run? Do you like having your poor knees all skinned up?"

"No, Mama," Amy had said. "I don't like skinned knees. I don't even like running really. I never used to run much before we came to Taylor Springs. But running is important in Taylor Springs. Everybody likes Betsey Rayburn just because she can beat everybody but Bert Miller at running."

Amy's mother had pushed a strand of pale hair back from her face and smiled sadly. "And being liked by everybody is more important than having scars and infections and worrying your mother, and—"

"No," Amy had interrupted. "That's not why I run—being liked, I mean. I run because—well, because sometimes I just have to. I don't know why."

But today she knew why. She had promised Aunt Abigail she would be home early and instead she was very late. When she reached the Hunter farm, she flung open the garden gate, raced up the path between Aunt Abigail's roses, and vaulted three steps at a time up the veranda stairs, landing lightly on her toes so no one would hear. But someone did hear, because just as she reached the door a voice said, "Amy," and she started guiltily before she realized that it was only her father. He was sitting in his wheelchair on the north veranda.

"Amy," Daniel Polonski called, "what's the big rush?" He took her hand and pulled her toward him, turning his dark whiskery cheek for a kiss. Around his eyes and forehead his skin had the purplish look that dark skin has when it fades from too little sunshine.

"I'm late," Amy said. "I promised Aunt Abigail I'd hurry home to help hoe the tomatoes."

"The tomatoes can wait a minute," her father said. "Sit down and talk a minute. What've you been up to today?" He was grinning, raising one bushy black eyebrow, making his thin stubbly face look cheerfully devilish, like a playful pirate.

Amy grinned back, tucking in her lips to make her dimple show. Her father liked dimples, and he liked to hear about things that made him laugh. Things like the system she had worked out for eating a licorice stick during arithmetic without anybody knowing, or the way she had hidden a puncture vine thorn in her hair, tucking it into the braid that Gordie Parks always yanked when he walked past her desk. Things like that made her father laugh and start telling about things he had done in school, and how he had been a holy terror when he was a boy, back in Chicago.

Hurriedly Amy tried to think of something her father would laugh about, but she couldn't think of anything. So she told him about Gordie and the new boy. She told him all about it except that she had done the tattling, because she knew that that was not the kind of thing he liked to hear. But she did say some things about Gordie Parks—what a stupid disgusting bully he was, and how much she hated him.

"Well now, Baby," her father said. "Don't be too hard on poor old Gordie. I've never had the pleasure of meeting the gentleman, myself, but he sounds to me pretty much like an ordinary, red-blooded American boy. In my day a new kid had to expect a few lickings, unless he was pretty good with his fists, or else pretty damn lucky. I remember one time when I—"

"Amy Abigail, I've been waiting for you for over

an hour." Aunt Abigail was standing on the path below the veranda, holding a hoe and dressed for gardening. "You're very late," she said.

Amy knew how late she was, but her guilty start was not so much for her lateness as for the "damn" her father had just said. If Aunt Abigail had arrived below the veranda in time to hear the damn, she would probably mention it and there would be another discussion about cursing.

"I'm coming, Aunt Abigail, right this minute. Just as soon as I change my clothes." Amy lunged for the door and got away before they could trap her in the middle of a discussion. She never liked hearing their discussions, because Aunt Abigail always won.

At one time, back in San Francisco, Amy's father had been very good at discussions. Amy could remember hearing him tell about discussions he had had, and won, with his friends at work, or even in the middle of big union meetings with dozens of people listening. Amy could remember sitting in the kitchen of their apartment on Franklin Street and listening to her father tell about discussions he had won, and jokes he had told with funny foreign accents that made everyone laugh. But no one could do very well in an argument with Aunt Abigail. And even when Amy knew that Aunt Abigail was right—with the Reverend Dawson, and the Bible, and probably even God on her side—she always felt sorry when her father lost.

But if there was a discussion that day it wasn't a very long one, because Aunt Abigail was already in the tomato patch when Amy dashed out the back door, still hooking the straps of her overalls. Aunt Abigail in the vegetable garden was a sight that took getting used to. Abigail Hunter gardened because of the Depression and because during hard times everyone had to make sacrifices, and also because hard work never hurt anybody. But no one seeing her in the garden would ever make the mistake of thinking she really belonged there.

Aunt Abigail had an old voile dress that she wore for gardening because it was cool and loose and didn't bind, and the long, flowing sleeves protected her arms from the sun. She wore gloves, too, old dress gloves that came up almost to the elbow, and a huge old motoring hat that she tied down with a long chiffon scarf. Her glasses were the pinch-on kind, and they quivered on the bridge of her nose with every stroke of the hoe, or bounced on her bosom on their silver chain. Except for her bosom, which was large and pigeon-shaped, Aunt Abigail was long and narrow and elegant-looking and she always managed to look her most elegant when she hoed weeds in the vegetable garden.

Luther Hunter, who had been Aunt Abigail's husband until he passed away, had owned the biggest farm in Taylor Valley; and back in the good times before the Depression, there had been several hired hands who lived and worked on the Hunter place all year-round—and many more who came for a while during the summer and harvest time. But now with bad times making it impossible to make a profit, most of the Hunter land was leased to cattle ranchers, and Aunt Abigail kept for herself only as much as she and Old Ike could take care of.

Old Ike, who had worked for the Hunters for a long, long time, was old and slow and nearly crippled in one leg, but he still milked the cows and tended the chickens and kept up the yard, so that the Hunter place always looked as neat and spruced up as ever, in spite of the hard times. Aunt Abigail insisted on that. But because hoeing was hard for Old Ike, she helped out in the vegetable garden.

Amy slowed down to time her approach so she arrived at the garden just as Aunt Abigail reached the end of a row. Working side by side up the next two rows, they would be able to talk, and Amy had a particular subject in mind.

But Aunt Abigail had something to say first. "Is this the way you hurry home, Miss?" she said.

"I'm sorry, Aunt Abigail," Amy said. "I *was* hurrying home 'til a new boy who lives in the Bradley place asked me to help him find the nest of a baby bird he'd found."

Amy knew the bird would be a good thing to mention. Aunt Abigail liked birds and had taught Amy a great deal about them.

"We found the nest," Amy said, "but it was in a hard place to reach, and it took a while to get the bird back in."

"Bradley place," Aunt Abigail said, thoughtfully. She straightened up, pushing against her back with one hand as if to shove the bend out. "Hmmm," she said. "Fitz-something or other. Doctor Fitz-something or other. Some kind of shirttail relatives of the Burtons. Heathens, according to your mother and the Reverend."

"Heathens?" Amy asked. "Who?"

"That bunch in the Bradley place. Your mother heard all about them from the Reverend Dawson. He called to invite them to services, and this Doctor Fitz-whatever told the Reverend that his wife was a Buddhist and he was an agnostic, or some such nonsense. Man's a writer, I hear."

"What's a Buddhist and an agnostic?" Amy asked.

"Heathens," her aunt said, bending back to her hoeing. "What's the child like?"

"The boy?" Amy stopped hoeing to think how to describe him. "He's strange-looking. I thought he was ugly at first, but he's not really. Just different-looking, with big eyes like an animal's and a bony kind of face. Alice says he's just plain crazy, and he does act awful strange in some ways. He's in my class, but he seems a lot younger—but in other ways he seems older. I don't know. He's hard to tell about, I guess."

Amy's answer didn't make much sense and she knew it, but it didn't make a whole lot of difference since Aunt Abigail didn't seem to be listening anyway. She'd gotten so far ahead while Amy puzzled over how to tell about Jason, that it took five minutes of furious hoeing to catch up. "How come they're living in the Bradley place?" she asked when she got close enough to talk.

"Well, the way I hear it," Aunt Abigail didn't stop hoeing this time, so her words came out punctuated with ladylike grunts at each stroke of the hoe. "This Mister or Doctor Fitzmaurice—I think they said—is a relative of old Mr. Burton. That's what the story is, at least, although I must say that I, for one, certainly didn't see any family likeness."

"You've seen them, then."

"I saw the man last Thursday at the market. Tall man, sharp-featured, with a little billy-goat beard like some kind of Bolshevik. Story is, he's working on some kind of history book and he wanted a quiet place to write and a chance to get the boy out into the country. He heard about the Bradley place through the Burtons. Must be pretty run down, standing empty for so long."

The mention of run-down houses reminded Amy of what she had meant to ask. "About old houses," she said, "I was wondering about the house in Stone Hollow. Tell me about it, Aunt Abigail. What happened there and why does everybody say it's haunted?"

"Haunted," Aunt Abigail snorted. "I've never met a haunt in my life, and I don't expect to. And you know as much about the Hollow as I do."

"Well, I know what the kids say, but they'll say anything. Like that little Bobby Parks says a man-eating cow lives in the Hollow."

"A man-eating what?"

Amy laughed. "A cow. He said he saw it. Coming up out of the Hollow with blood all over it where it had been eating people."

Aunt Abigail made a snorting noise. "I've been hearing stories about the Hollow all my life, but that's the wildest one I've heard yet," she said.

"What are some of the other ones? The ones you've heard all your life."

"Now, you know I don't hold with that kind of nonsense, Amy Abigail," Aunt Abigail said. "Just as you said, you can hear anything if you've a mind to listen. 'Specially in a backwoods place like Taylor Springs. But there's not a thing that can't be explained without having to bring any hocus-pocus into it. There are perfectly reasonable causes behind everything that ever happened there. Even what happened to that poor Italian family is just what might have been expected."

"They were the ones that built the shack, weren't they? Tell me about them, Aunt Abigail. What happened to the poor Italian family?"

"Nobody knows exactly. Except they had a little

girl die of the lockjaw and not long afterward the father died, too, in an accident. They say someone from the town went up and found the man dead, just outside the barn, and the woman was missing. They found her later wandering in the Hills, and sent her away to an asylum. They say she was as mad as a March Hare. Those that found her spread all sorts of wild tales about the things she said, but sensible people didn't pay any attention. Downright sinful to frighten people with the ravings of a madwoman."

"But why did she go mad, Aunt Abigail?"

"Who knows why a person goes mad. Not that it was to be wondered at, losing her husband and little girl so close together that way. With all that grief to bear, and being Italian to begin with, it would have been almost more of a wonder if she hadn't gone crazy." Aunt Abigail stopped again to straighten her back.

"Do Italians go crazy easier than other people?" Amy asked.

"Well, I don't know about that, but they are a flighty bunch. Apt to fly off the handle about most anything. Catholics, you know. The whole bunch of them."

Amy had heard Aunt Abigail so many times on the subject of the Catholics that she was sure she already knew all the interesting facts by heart, so she tried to steer the conversation back to Stone Hollow.

"But some other people died up in the Hills, too,

didn't they, Aunt Abigail?"

Aunt Abigail shrugged. "Just a couple of boot-leggers. They'd built a still up there to make whiskey."

"But what did they die of?"

"Nobody knows for sure. Probably killed each other. Got drunk on some of their own whiskey and got into a fight about something. Nothing very mysterious about that."

Then, before Amy could try again for new information on Stone Hollow, Aunt Abigail switched the conversation back to the Catholics and refused to change. Amy wasn't very interested, since she had heard it all so many times before, but at least this time her father wasn't around to hear it. Daniel Polonski had been born a Catholic, and although he said he wasn't much of anything anymore, he didn't like to hear the things that Aunt Abigail always said about them. When her aunt and her father started discussing the Catholics, Amy usually tried to be someplace else.

Aunt Abigail had gotten sidetracked off the Catholics and had started in on the Unitarians—who according to her were just as bad, only different—when the approach of Old Ike provided an interruption. Amy had noticed him coming across the farmyard for a long time before he arrived. He walked slowly, dragging his stiff left leg, and frowning more and more fiercely the closer he came, until his thick gray eyebrows seemed to meet over his hooked beak of a nose. Following, as he always did, several yards behind, came Ike's old gray dog, Caesar.

"Miz Abigail," Old Ike began, "think I better take the Jersey over to Rayburns' today or tomorrow—" before Aunt Abigail interrupted him.

"Amy Abigail," she said, "run along for a minute. Run along and—" She glanced around looking for something to tell Amy to do. "—and cheer up that poor old dog. He looks about as happy as a cat in a mud puddle."

Amy was glad for a chance to play with old Caesar instead of hoeing tomatoes, although she would have liked to stay and listen. Not so much to hear about taking the Jersey cow to see Mr. Rayburn's bull— she'd already found out all about that from Betsey Rayburn—but just because Old Ike himself was one of the things she needed to find out more about. There was something strange and mysterious about so many years of scowling silence, and Amy had something inside that made her have to find out about anything that seemed the least bit secret. For as long as she could remember, there had always been things that she just had to know about, and Old Ike was one of those things.

She left, slowly looking back over her shoulder, until it became obvious that neither Old Ike nor Aunt Abigail was going to say anything until she was completely out of earshot.

"Caesar," Amy said plaintively, as she approached

the old dog, "aren't you even a little bit glad to see me?" As usual, he was pretending he wasn't. His head was turned away, and he was trying to pretend that he was very interested in watching an old brown hen that was scratching in the dust near the wood-shed. But he was really watching Amy out of the corner of his eye.

Amy squatted down right in front of him and made her voice sad and trembly. "Don't you like me just a tiny little bit?"

He broke down then, as he always did, and pressed against her, licking her face with his warm wet tongue, and wagging his thin tail. She put her arms around him and hugged, and he stood very still with his eyes almost closed and made a croony noise deep in his throat. Once, when Amy's mother had heard him do that, she had jerked Amy away from him in fright, not understanding that that growl had nothing to do with biting. But Amy understood. It was easy to see why a dog who'd belonged to Old Ike for years and years would understand growling better than anything else. And poor old Caesar *was* Ike's dog, at least as much as he belonged to anybody.

When the old man limped past Amy on his way to the barn, Caesar pulled away and followed him. But he stopped twice to look back at Amy and flap his skinny tail.

chapter three

That evening Amy was still thinking about Stone Hollow. Although she had long ago questioned everyone who might know anything about it, she was suddenly tormented with an inescapable itch to find out more, to see if anybody had any scrap of information that she might somehow have missed about the mysterious hidden valley.

The next person she had a chance to question was her father, during their regular before-dinner game of checkers. With her aunt and mother busy in the kitchen, she had a perfect opportunity, so she took it, even though her father was not a very good prospect, being almost a stranger to Taylor Springs.

A stranger, Amy thought, looking at her father's dark, sharp-edged face, shadowed now as he bent over the checkerboard. A stranger to Taylor Springs. It was odd, but that was what he seemed, even though he had lived there as long—a little longer, really—than Amy had herself. Yet Amy had always thought of herself as a Taylor Springs person. Even before she had ever been there, she had thought of herself as somehow belonging to Taylor Springs.

"How much longer have you lived in Taylor Springs than I have, Daddy?" she asked.

"Longer?" her father said. "Oh, you mean when I came here in '25 to work on the bridge and met your mother?"

Amy nodded.

"Well, let's see. I started work around the first of April, but I stayed in Lambertville the first week or two and drove up every day, until I found a room in Taylor Springs. And your mother and I left town on the twenty-eighth of September. We were married in Reno that evening, and the next day we hit out for San Francisco. And that was the last I saw of the great little town of Taylor Springs 'til we came back to live with your Aunt Abigail two years ago last May."

"Why did you and Mama go to Reno to get married?" Amy asked. "Why didn't you get married right here in our own church?"

"Well now, Amy Abigail," her father said, "I think you know the answer to that question."

Even without the twisted grin and the tilted eyebrow, Amy would have known her father was being

34

sarcastic. He never called her Amy Abigail except when he meant it to be sarcastic.

"And if you don't, you'd best ask your mother about it, or your Aunt Abigail. Your Aunt Abigail would be a good one to ask about that."

Of course Amy had already asked and, just as her father said, she did know the reason, more or less. She knew that her mother had been living on the Hunter farm with Aunt Abigail when she met and married Daniel Polonski, and that Aunt Abigail had not approved of the marriage. What Amy didn't really know was why. Once at school, Shirley Anderson had told Amy that her mother said Helen Fairchild had run away to get married because her sister and her fiancé had had an awful fight. Amy had asked about that, too.

"Fight?" Aunt Abigail had answered. "That Mary Anderson was born gossiping, and her daughter's just like her. That's the trouble with a place like Taylor Springs—nothing better to do with your time. When you hear malicious stories like that, you have to consider the source, Amy Abigail. Consider the source."

"Fight? Your auntie and me?" Amy's father had laughed. "Why, in those days, Baby, I weighed in at two hundred pounds and could have licked my weight in wildcats. Wouldn't have been a very fair match, would it, for me to fight with a lady? Not even your Aunt Abigail."

When Amy saw that he wasn't going to be serious,

she had tried her mother. What she asked her mother was, "Did Aunt Abigail and Daddy have an awful fight about you and him getting married, Mama? Is that why you went away to get married and never came back until Daddy broke his back and couldn't work anymore so you had to come back and live with Aunt Abigail or else go on relief? That's what Shirley Anderson says that her mother says."

Amy's mother's answer had been, "What, dear? Who said that? Why, I can't imagine where she heard a thing like that. Your father and I went away because he had a job waiting for him in San Francisco, and we never came back until after he was hurt because he was so busy and working so hard. Your father always had to work so hard. He did such hard dangerous work. I was always so worried about him. Bridges are such dangerous things. Why even the little bridge to Lambertville where he was working when we first met—"

"When we first met," her mother said, and the answer about whether there had been a fight turned into a story that Amy had heard many times before. A story about the tall handsome young man who came to Taylor Springs, and how all the girls had admired him, but how he had only paid attention to Helen Fairchild, who was still blond and beautiful then, even though she was already a little older than most girls are when they marry, and who some of the younger girls already thought of as an old maid. And exactly what the handsome young man was doing when they first met, and what they said to each other, and what they said the next time they met, and on and on and on. Amy had always liked the story, but it didn't really answer the question.

"I have asked, Daddy," Amy said. "I asked about why you went away to get married."

"And what did they say?"

"Mama told me all about how handsome you were when you met, and Aunt Abigail said Mary Anderson was a born gossip."

They both laughed, and then Amy remembered the other question, the one she had intended to ask her father before it was time for dinner.

"Daddy," she said, "what kinds of things have you heard about Stone Hollow? I know you haven't ever been there, but haven't you heard people talking about it?"

"Stone Hollow?" her father said, looking for a moment as if he didn't even know what she was talking about. But then he remembered. "Oh, yeah," he said. "You mean that place up in the Hills where some bootleggers had a still during Prohibition?"

"Yes," Amy said, "and where an Italian family had a farm only something happened to them, and now everyone says it's haunted and everything? Have you heard about it? Anything more, I mean?"

"More than what?" her father said, grinning. "Seems to me you know quite a bit already. Seems to me, as a matter of fact, that nearly everything I know about the place is what you've told me. That is, except for—"

"Except for what, Daddy?"

"Well, now that I think about it, it does seem to me that Ike mentioned it a while back."

"Really? What did he say?"

"Oh, I don't know. Nothing that made much sense. I just asked him what kind of hooch they made up there. Seemed to me that living so close, and liking a nip now and then as much as Ike does, that he would have given the local product at least a try."

"But what did he say?"

"Not much. Just stared at me for a moment and then started saying No he didn't know, and No he hadn't tried it, and No he didn't know anything about it. So I dropped it, but then after a minute he looked around as if he thought someone might be listening, and then he whispered something about how it could have been good stuff, the very best, and how they could have made a million if they hadn't started playing with fire."

"Who, Daddy? Who was playing with fire?"

"Can't tell you. He wouldn't say any more. When I tried to bring it up again, he just muttered something about 'evil' and walked off."

"What do you suppose he meant?"

"Don't know. Except everyone around here seems to think that that valley is haunted by some kind of evil spirits. Guess Old Ike believes it, too."

That was all her father could tell her, and that left only her mother to be questioned again. However, her mother was apt to be the best possibility. On most subjects that had to do with Taylor Springs, Helen Fairchild Polonski was a walking storehouse of information. It seemed almost certain that somewhere in the back of her memory, she was sure to have an almost forgotten bit of information about Stone Hollow. Amy's chance to find out came after dinner when Aunt Abigail left the dishes to Amy and her mother because President Roosevelt was talking on the radio. Aunt Abigail didn't think much of President Roosevelt because he had voted against Prohibition, but she always liked to listen to him on the radio.

"Mama," Amy began, "Aunt Abigail and I were talking about the things that happened at Stone Hollow, but she didn't remember very much. You always remember so much about everything that happened a long time ago, I was wondering if you remember any special things you heard about the Hollow. Like, why everybody is so sure it's haunted. Do you remember anything special about that?"

"Stone Hollow? Well, let me see." Helen Polonski drifted away from the dishpan and came to rest on the edge of a kitchen chair. As she thought, she dried her hands over and over again on her apron. Her face always seemed to soften when she was remembering, blurring out the hard thin lines and webs of wrinkles.

"The first thing I recall hearing talk about was the Ranzoni family," she said. "That was when I was just a little girl. But it seems to me I remember hearing our papa say that people were afraid of the Hollow even before that. Something about the Indians. The Indians used to have meetings there, I think, some kind of heathen religious ceremonies. But that might have been just a rumor."

"Did you ever go up there, Mama?"

"Oh no," her mother said. "We weren't allowed. And I would never have gone without Papa's permission." She reached up to push a wisp of pale hair away from her cheek, and her mouth curved into a faint smile. Amy knew the smile well. It went with Helen Polonski's memories of her childhood, a childhood that Amy had heard so much about that sometimes it seemed more real than her own. Growing up in an apartment and on city streets, cool, fog-bound streets where the air tasted of ocean and faraway places, Amy had had a second childhood in a hot, golden valley in the Sierra foothills. Long before she had ever really seen it, Amy had played under its huge shade trees, visited the families in its old wooden houses, and walked in the shadow of its encircling hills.

Long before Amy had ever met the children at Taylor Springs School whose names were Lewis, Harris, Parks, Paulsen and Rayburn, she knew a great many things about their parents and grandparents and aunts and uncles. She knew who had been hardworking and God-fearing and churchgoing, and who, on the other hand, had been proud and worldly, or ignorant and lazy. She even knew about a few who had been "no better than they ought to be" and even one or two who were "scandalous," although she had never been able to find out exactly what they had done to get that way.

Amy had loved hearing the stories. "Tell me about the hayride and Bertie Lewis," she would ask her mother, or "tell me about the big flood." And Helen Polonski would sit down at the kitchen table in their apartment on Franklin Street, and her face would get soft and blurry, and they would go back to the time when a hayride was almost turned into a tragedy by a reckless boy—or to the January when the river flooded and Amy's grandfather, the Reverend Fairchild, worked all night in the rain to help save the belongings of some Mexican families who had built their shacks too near the river.

Sometimes Amy still liked to hear the stories, even now that she lived in Taylor Springs and found it strangely unlike her imaginings. But on this particular evening she was interested only in her mother's memories about one particular thing.

"But didn't you ever get close to the Hollow?" she asked. "Didn't you ever climb to the top of the ridge where the road starts down and you can see the house and what's left of the sheds and barn?"

"No, I didn't. Some of the children did, I know. But Papa didn't want us to go so far into the Hills. Of course, he didn't believe all the stories about ghosts and hauntings, but he felt there were better things for us to do with our time. I do think that Abigail might have gone once, as far as the hilltop."

"Did she see the house? What did it look like then? Did it still have doors and windows?"

Suddenly Amy's mother looked at her sharply. "Have you been there?" she asked.

"Oh no," Amy said quickly. "Not all the way there. But I've been as far as the ridge. Remember that time last summer when Alice and I made a picnic lunch and went hiking? We were going up Bradley Lane and we just happened to notice where the road to the Hollow began, and we followed it, but only as far as the ridge. We started to eat our lunch right there on the ridge, only we didn't because we saw something."

"Something?" her mother asked, leaning forward from where she was still sitting on the very edge of her chair. "What kind of something?"

"Well, I don't know for sure," Amy said. It was the second time that day that she had told about the thing that had moved in the shadow of the oak tree near the shack, but this time she was more careful not to add any interesting details that might not have been there for sure. "It was whitish," she said, "and it kind of swayed back and forth—"

42

But, even so, her mother's face tightened with concern.

"Amy Abigail," she said reproachfully, "are you remembering—"

"Mama," Amy said. "I'm *not* exaggerating. I'm not. We did see a white thing. You can ask Alice. We both saw it, and we both ran. We thought it was a ghost."

"A ghost," her mother said. "That sounds like heathen talk. You know we don't believe in ghosts, goblins, and nonsense like that."

"But we believe in spirits, don't we?" Amy said. "Like in the Bible where Jesus made the evil spirits go into the herd of swine."

"Devils," Helen Polonski nodded. "Devils, yes, but not misty white things that rap on tables and float through doors. That kind of thing is just spiritualist—"

Just then Aunt Abigail returned to the kitchen to fill her teacup, and Amy's mother jumped up and hurried back to the dishpan.

"Are spiritualist what, Mama?" Amy asked.

"Nonsense," her mother said. "Heathen spiritualist nonsense."

"Nonsense?" Aunt Abigail asked. "What's nonsense?" She took a kettle that Amy was drying out of her hands and inspected the bottom. The shiny metal was smudged here and there with black sooty smears.

"Oh, didn't I remember to scour—" Amy's mother began, as she reached for the kettle, but Aunt Abigail shouldered her aside and began to scrub furiously.

"Here, let me. I'll do it, Abigail," Amy's mother said, nervously trying to catch the drips that fell from her wet fingers.

Amy handed the dish towel to her mother and backed away, watching and listening. Listening to all the talk about a small smudge on the bottom of a kettle, Amy was getting the feeling that her aunt and mother were really talking about something else—something different, and more important and more secret.

She often got that feeling—that when grown-ups talked about lots of little unimportant things, they were really talking about secrets that were somehow connected to things that had happened a long time before. Sometimes Amy had the feeling that she was surrounded by secrets and the clues to secrets, and that it was really important that she find out more about them. But there weren't many clues in the talk about the kettle bottom, so she kept on backing up until she was out of the room and partway up the back stairs.

Halfway up she began to run, two steps at a time, and the last three in a mighty jump. Then down the hall, still running, but quietly so they wouldn't hear her and say what they always said.

"It's so unladylike, Amy, and dangerous. Just look at your poor knees."

"Amy Abigail, how many times do I have to ask you

not to run in the house. You'll break something."

"Let her run, for God's sake. Not much else she's allowed to do."

Amy's room in Aunt Abigail's house was small with a sloping ceiling and cubbyholed dormer windows. She liked its smallness and the sleek polished shine of the floor and the high carved headboard of the old-fashioned bed. She liked the narrow windows that opened right into the branches of one of the enormous pepper trees, so that the whole room was full of cool green light and the sounds of wind and birds. She liked having the tree there, except when she would have liked to see past it, to the Old Road and beyond to where the Hills rose up against the sky.

For a moment Amy stood at the window, staring out into a thick green curtain of leaves, and then she turned and tiptoed out of her room and down the hall.

chapter four

From the Hunter house, the view of the eastern hills was blocked by the row of pepper trees, except from one window in one upstairs room. And it was to that room that Amy was going, although it was a place that she was not supposed to visit by herself.

It was known as the storeroom because, for many years, Aunt Abigail had used it for storing away all kinds of keepsakes, and things that she was not using at present but might need again someday. It was a lonely place, standing alone and untouched sometimes for weeks at a time, and it smelled slightly of dust and of something else more subtle and mysterious. It was a musty smell, sweet but sad, like the smell of decaying rose petals, and Amy thought of it as seeping up from bundles of old letters and from tissue-wrapped packets of things like baby dresses and wedding veils.

The furniture that had been exiled to the storeroom was old and out of style. Some of it had once belonged to the Hunter family, but much of it had come from the Fairchild parsonage. There was a desk that had belonged to Amy's grandmother, a lady's desk, carved and ornamented, but too small to be useful to Aunt Abigail, who had farm records to keep and household business to take care of. Someday, Aunt Abigail said, the desk would be Amy's.

Next to the desk was an ancient rosewood dresser with a marble top and next to it a clumsy old highboy with many glass-paned doors. Then came rocking chairs, bookcases, lamps, and whatnot cabinets and, all along one wall, a row of large boxes and old-fashioned dome-lidded trunks.

From time to time Amy had been allowed to accompany her aunt or mother when they went into the storeroom to put something away or just to dust and clean. A few other times, she had spent hours there with her mother, going through some of the old trunks. Together they had looked at old china-headed dolls with kid leather bodies, tarnished silver spoons, and fancy baby dresses. In a box marked *School Days*, they had found dozens of old report cards, and fancy certificates awarded for Sunday School attendance, or Bible verses memorized, or good handwriting. Another trunk was almost entirely full of old photographs. There were hundreds of photographs, sorted into large envelopes, or neatly mounted in albums with puffy velvet covers. It took hours to look through all the photographs, because Amy's mother knew a story to go with almost every one.

One of the first pictures in the fanciest old album was a favorite of Amy's. It was a wedding picture, the wedding of Amy's grandfather and grandmother. Amy's grandfather, with a darker beard and hair but otherwise looking much the same as he did in all his other pictures, was standing stiff and straight beside a chair in which his bride was sitting, dressed in a beautiful white dress with a long lacy veil.

Looking at that picture always gave Amy an interesting feeling—a curious feeling, beautiful and exciting, but very sad. It was sad to look at someone so young and smiling, and know that the person had died so soon afterward, leaving two little girls without a mother. And what made it seem especially tragic, so tragic that Amy could get a tight feeling in her throat just thinking about it, was the fact that she had been so very beautiful—and that her name had been Amy. Looking at her picture made Amy wonder about things—things like being beautiful, and dying.

Once when she had been in the storeroom alone, she had put the album down and, going over to the mirror on the rosewood dresser, she had pulled the back of her skirt up over her head like a veil and smiled, trying to make her face warm, blond, and glowing, like that other Amy's had been when she had her picture taken for her wedding, on June the twenty-first, 1896, in Des Moines, Iowa.

There were not many other pictures of Amy's grandmother in the albums, and in the few there were, she looked much different from the way she did in the wedding picture. In one labeled *Abigail 2 years, Helen 6 months*, she was shown sitting in a rocking chair holding two babies on her lap. In that picture the other Amy's blond hair was pulled back close to her head and her face looked blurred and faded.

"There we are, Abigail and I, when we were just babies," Amy's mother had said when she showed Amy the picture. "Just look at those curls."

"Is that your mama?" Amy had asked.

"Why, yes, of course."

"She looks so different from the way she looks in the other picture."

Amy's mother had held the picture to the light and examined it carefully. "Yes, she does," she said. "I suppose she wasn't very well when the picture was taken. She was never very well after they came to Taylor Springs. She died when I was only six years old, you know. I don't remember her much at all, but Abigail does. Abigail remembers her very well."

"Wasn't it awful?" Amy asked. "Wasn't it terrible to have your mama die when you were so little?"

"Yes," her mother said. "It was very sad. But I was

so young at the time that I don't think I really understood what had happened. I don't remember much about how I felt at the time. And we were very fortunate to have such a wonderful father. Even though we had lost our mother, Abigail and I were never neglected for a moment. Our papa saw to that."

Amy's mother usually spoke of her father as "our papa," and she spoke of him a lot. Although he had died three years before Amy was born, she always felt as if she had known him. Through her mother's stories, she had heard all about the Reverend Jeremiah Fairchild who had come to Taylor Springs in 1896 with his young wife, and who had built a church and guided the lives, not only of his own family, but of the whole community for thirty-seven years. He had been a very important man in Taylor Springs, and all of the picture albums in Aunt Abigail's storeroom were full of pictures of him. In some of the pictures he was doing important things like dedicating the new schoolhouse or giving a talk at the Fourth of July picnic. And in all of the pictures he looked very much the same, tall and dignified with a face like the face of a statue, handsome and dignified and unsmiling.

Amy spent almost as much time looking at the pictures of her grandfather as she did the ones of her grandmother, but they gave her a very different feeling. While the pictures of her poor young grandmother Amy made her feel sad in a rather pleasant romantic way, the ones of her grandfather were somehow a little frightening. She didn't know why, exactly, except that it seemed so impossible that such an important and determined-looking person would allow his plans to be interrupted by dying. There were times when, looking up from his pictures, Amy almost expected to see him standing in the door of the store-room, wearing a long dark coat and a stern and dignified expression.

When Amy reached the door of the storeroom, she stopped for a moment and listened carefully to be sure that no one was coming up the stairs. Aunt Abigail had never in so many words forbidden Amy to go to the room alone, probably because it never occurred to her that she would want to, but her mother had warned her about it. Aunt Abigail was very particular, she said, about everything being put back in exactly the right place. So, Amy reasoned, it wouldn't matter as long as she put everything back in just the right place. Actually, she really knew she shouldn't go there. It was just that she couldn't seem to help it. She didn't know what it was that made the store-room so strangely irresistible, except that she had a mysterious feeling that somewhere in the crowded room was something, or perhaps a lot of things, that she needed to find out about.

She had been in the storeroom many times without finding out anything very important, but that was not surprising since she didn't know where to look, or even exactly what she was looking for. For a while she thought perhaps the desk, or one of the other pieces of old furniture, might have a secret drawer or compartment that would fly open if she found the hidden spring and reveal—a treasure, or perhaps an important secret document. At other times she felt the clue might be found in the bundles of old letters or postcards, or even in the pictures in one of the photograph albums.

She had already discovered a small clue to some kind of mystery concerning one of the old photographs. One day, when she and her mother were looking through the albums, Aunt Abigail had appeared in the doorway just as Amy found a beautiful picture of two little girls dressed in fancy high-necked dresses, standing hand in hand on the front steps of the Taylor Springs church. The picture was labeled *Abigail and Helen Fairchild—ages 8 and 6.*

"Look, Aunt Abigail," Amy had said, bringing her the album. "Look at you and Mama. Look at the big hair ribbons and the beautiful dresses."

But Aunt Abigail had only glanced at the picture briefly, shaking her head and smiling a strange, almost angry smile. As she handed it back, she said something under her breath that sounded like, "Poor little puppets." She walked away then, but when Amy had questioned her mother about it, she had learned very little.

"Did she say that?" Amy's mother had said. "Are

you sure? I can't imagine what she meant by that. I can't imagine—" But then she sat for a long time fingering the edges of the album and looking at the picture of the two little girls who had been Abigail and Helen Fairchild. After a while she said, almost as if she were talking to herself, "Abigail was not a happy child. Sometimes I think she—" But then she looked at Amy and hushed suddenly and began to talk quickly about another picture—as if there were something secret about what she had started to say.

There was something secret about what was, and wasn't, said that day and, if there was a secret, it was obvious that Aunt Abigail had the answers. But Aunt Abigail, Amy had soon discovered, did *not* like to talk about *her* childhood. So the secret had remained a secret and became one more in the long list of things that Amy needed to find out about—one more answer that might be waiting right there among the hundreds of bits and pieces of the past that had waited through the years in Aunt Abigail's storeroom.

But on this particular evening as Amy tiptoed through the door of the storeroom, she was not so much interested in the contents of the room itself. As soon as she had carefully and noiselessly closed the door behind her, she made her way as directly as possible to a steamer trunk that sat below the window. Climbing up on the trunk, she rolled up the window shade, and there they were. Rising up into a pink-tinged sky, the Hills loomed high, and then higher, an endless labyrinth of crests and canyons, lonely, mysterious, and forbidding.

"He couldn't have," she whispered after a while. "He couldn't have all by himself. Nobody is as brave as that."

chapter five

He came out of the clump of eucalyptus trees again the next morning when she was on her way to school. But although he appeared with startling suddenness from behind the tree trunks, Amy's reaction was not so much fright as embarrassment. She was embarrassed because he might have noticed that she was acting strangely. Actually, she had been playing a game.

It was a long way from the Hunter farm to Taylor Springs School, and Amy had thought up a lot of different ways to entertain herself along the way. All the games had something to do with traveling or making long journeys. There was Camel Caravan on the Sahara, Cattle Drive on the Santa Fe Trail, and even the Children's Crusade. Today, though, it had been one of her favorites, Gold Rush Pi

Amy glared at Jason, thinking back o
what had just happened in the game. Sin
around the bend in the road, she had be
the desert, and she couldn't remember doing anything more than cracking a whip and maybe staggering a little—as if walking in deep sand. But if Jason
noticed either the whipping or staggering, he didn't
mention it.

After he emerged suddenly, almost at her elbow,
and before she had recovered from her embarrassment
enough to think of a way to prevent it, he started
walking beside her. Amy walked faster, and he hurried
to keep up like a baby goose frantically following anything that moved because it might be its mother. She
was trying to think of a way to tell him to go away,
when he said, "I went there again last night."

"You went where?" she said, and then stopped
dead. "Not to the Hollow. You didn't go to the
Hollow at night?"

"Not exactly. Twilight. I left there before it was
actually dark."

"Good heavens," Amy said. "You really are crazy.
Did anything happen?"

He nodded. "The wind blew in circles," he said.
"And there were noises—voices maybe. There would
have been more, I think, if I had stayed."

Amy shivered. Surely he was lying, but he lied so
well—with only a thoughtful remembering expression

—as if he were trying carefully to recall every detail correctly—and there was no sneaky watching for Amy's reaction. She turned and walked on wondering.

He walked beside her silently for a while before he said, "Are you going away soon?"

She knew what he meant, but she pretended not to. "Going away? Where to? Why should I be going away?"

"Away to live. You said you were visiting your aunt. Will you be going back to San Francisco when your father gets well?"

"He won't get well," Amy said. "At least he won't be able to walk again. But when the Depression is over, he's going to get an office job where he can work sitting down, and we'll go back then. But there are no jobs now even if he took the training. He's tried and tried to get a job. He even paid a lawyer to try. The lawyer tried to make the company where my father got his back broken give him an office job. But they didn't have a job either. But as soon as the Depression gets better, my father says he'll study bookkeeping, and we'll go back to San Francisco, except—"

"Except what?"

"Oh nothing. I was just going to say that my aunt doesn't think my father will be able to get a job." Then to change the subject, she asked, "How long are you going to stay?"

"I don't know. But it won't be for very long. Just 'til my father finishes his book." He stopped suddenly and picked up a smooth, shiny stone. "Look at this," he said. "It looks like a prayer stone."

"A what?"

"A prayer stone. They're usually found near sacred rivers. They have special powers."

"Powers? What kind of powers?"

"Supernatural powers," Jason said. He put the stone in his pocket.

"Oh," Amy said. "We don't believe in stuff like that."

"You don't?" Jason seemed surprised. "You mean you've never met a person who had supernatural powers?"

"No, I haven't."

"That's strange," Jason said. He trotted a ways to keep up with Amy's fast walk. "Do you like it here?" he asked.

"Like it here? In Taylor Springs? Of course I like it here!" But even as she said it, a memory came of closed tight faces and turned backs. She had begun to forget how it was to be new at Taylor Springs School where everyone had known each other since they were babies and knew exactly what to do and what was expected. She had begun to forget how she had come with such high hopes—feeling as if she were coming home to the place where she belonged—and then found that she didn't seem a part of things, without knowing why or what she could do about it. It had been a terrible and frightening time.

But she had learned quickly. She had set herself to learn how to belong at Taylor Springs School, and she had been successful. But remembering how it had been made her feel frightened, and the fright quickly turned into anger. "Why shouldn't I like it here?" she demanded.

"I don't know," he said. "It's just that you're so different—"

"Different? I'm not either different. What do you mean I'm different?" But just then she noticed how close they were getting to the school grounds, so she didn't wait for an answer. She was not about to walk into the schoolyard with this crazy Jason. In Taylor Springs girls walked to school alone or with other girls. And certainly not with a crazy new boy. She'd never hear the last of it, if she did that.

Stopping in her tracks, she frowned at Jason fiercely and said, "Go on. Go on to school. I have to do something first."

But he only smiled his dumb gosling smile and said, "I'll wait for you."

"No you won't! I don't want to walk with you. Now go on."

The smile went, and left his face limp and defenseless, as it had been after Gordie's fist. He walked away leaving Amy wanting to call after him and tell him that it was only that girls didn't walk to school with boys at Taylor Springs. She felt rotten and guilty, the way she did when she put off something her mother had asked her to do, until her mother, sighing sadly, did it herself. She hated the feeling, and because he had no right to make her feel that way, she yelled after him, "Don't ever talk to me again."

No one called him Jason at school that day except Miss McMillan. Everyone else called him Sissy, because he still wouldn't hit back when Gordie hit him. And Gordie hit him all the time. Gordie said he had a special reason because he had had to stay after school for swearing, and that was Jason's fault. But Gordie didn't really need any special reason. After he'd gotten even for the staying-after, he went on hitting Jason for no reason at all. He tripped him in the hall, banged into his desk and spilled his milk during lunch hour, and even stuck him with a pencil as he walked by him during class. Watching, Amy began to feel more and more angry—angry at Miss McMillan for not seeing anything, and at Gordie for being such an idiot bully, and most of all at Jason himself for being so sickeningly helpless, like a wounded mouse in the clutches of a tormenting cat.

By afternoon everyone was talking about what Gordie was going to do to the new boy after school. Gordie was telling everyone that he was going to wait in the bushes until the sissy came by on his way home from school. By three o'clock everyone in the room knew about it, except Miss McMillan and Jason himself.

When the dismissal bell rang in Miss McMillan's

class, you cleaned up your desk and then raised your hand for the desk monitor to come around and inspect. If your desk was clean enough, you were dismissed. Watching Jason stacking a pile of books and papers on the corner of his desk so he could wipe it out with a paper towel, Amy suddenly wadded up a scrap of something and started with it to the wastepaper basket. On the way she brushed against Jason's desk and shoved his things off onto the floor. Everyone who saw it grinned, knowing she'd done it on purpose. Then she went back to her desk and carefully arranged and rearranged her own books. By the time Jason had picked up his books and all the scattered pieces of paper, they were the only ones left in the room. Then Amy went to the cloakroom and stayed there, waiting.

He came at last and seeing her he started to smile, but she grabbed his arm and whispered at him fiercely.

"Stay here for a minute," she hissed. "Then look out the door. I'll be out by the swings. If I'm swinging, go back in and wait a while longer, but if I'm just standing there, come on out and run down and wait behind the janitor's shed. Okay?"

Jason stared blankly for just a moment before his face convulsed into his babyishly eager smile. "All right," he said. "I'll wait for your signal, and then I'll advance to the next rendezvous." And then as Amy turned to go, he whispered, "What are we playing?"

"Playing?" Amy said. "We're not playing anything. Gordie's laying for you, that's all."

She ran out quickly, before his smile had time to disappear.

The schoolyard seemed to be empty, but Amy checked the driveway and the front steps to see if Gordie had posted any spies before she made her way to the swings. Waiting there, she saw the door to Miss McMillan's room open. Jason came out, looked in her direction, and then ran toward the shed. Amy followed slowly, looking carefully around for any sign of spies or watchers. She was taking a risk. Not only Gordie, but also a lot of the others, would give her trouble if they found out. She didn't really know why she was doing it. Except that she hated Gordie, and the new boy was so—helpless. She pictured him cowering behind the shed, waiting for her to come and tell him what to do.

Only he wasn't. When she reached the shed, he bounded out at her and said, "Advance and give the password."

Amy frowned. "Look. I told you, it's no game. Gordie and some other guys are waiting for you somewhere along the road. But I know a way you may get past them. It's kind of a long-cut down the riverbed and then up across the Paulsens' orchard. It comes out halfway down Bradley Lane. You ought to be all right if you get that far without getting caught."

She started off fast not looking at him or speaking.

It was strange; he didn't seem grateful that she was helping him, or even too scared. It was as if he were just too dumb to realize what would have happened if she hadn't. As if he didn't realize, too, what would happen to *her* if anybody found out. Most of the kids wouldn't hit her, the way Gordie might, but they had other ways of letting you know when you had done something you were not supposed to do. And one of those things was siding with a stranger against your friends. Amy walked quickly, looking back from time to time and frowning, so Jason wouldn't try to walk beside her and talk.

By the time they reached the riverbed, and were picking their way among the rocks between the cliff and the edge of the water, he had stopped trying to talk to her. He was walking several yards behind, and before long he began to act very strangely. Glancing back over her shoulder, Amy saw him walking on tiptoe, and then dropping to his knees from time to time and staring at the ground. She walked more slowly and at last stopped.

"What were you doing?" she asked when he caught up.

"Doing?" he said. "Oh, back there? That was an Indian. Sometimes I'm an Indian guide."

"Oh?" Thinking she understood, Amy nodded, relieved that that was all, but puzzled and amused that he didn't seem at all embarrassed to admit it. It had been years since she had admitted to anyone about

64

things like that, things she still did—like Gold Rush Pioneers or Camel Caravan. If she still played pretending games in the sixth grade she, at least, had enough sense not to let anyone know. "Oh," she said again, making a teasing smile. "You were playing Indian. Do you play cowboy sometimes, too?"

"It's not playing, exactly." Jason said. He sounded serious, not teased or angry, but thoughtful. "Not playing. I really become an Indian, sometimes. It's something a friend of mine in Greece taught me how to do."

Amy could only stare, bewildered and then angry. "You were *playing!*" she said. "Look! You don't have to lie to me. I do it, too. All the time." She hadn't meant to tell, but it had slipped out because she was angry. He kept doing that—making her get angry and do things she hadn't planned or meant to do.

At least he didn't tease back. He only looked interested and asked her how she did it. And somehow, there they were, walking along the riverbed, side by side, while Amy told him about the Pioneer game—how she usually played it, and how it was based on a book she read once about a girl whose father had gone west with the gold rush and had never been heard from since, and how the girl was on her way west with a pioneer train to see if she could find him.

At a spot where the cliff was low, a narrow path led up from the riverbed to a part of the Paulsen ranch. They climbed the cliff together, still talking. It turned out that Jason had read a lot about the pioneers, too. He knew about the Jumping-Off Place and the Santa Fe Trail and the Donner party and even things that Amy wasn't too sure about, like which Indian tribes were friendly and which were not. They were discussing whether horses or mules or oxen were best to pull covered wagons when they reached the top of the low hill on which the Paulsens' orchard had been planted. From that vantage point, the part of the Old Road that curved west around the Paulsen land could be seen. At the end of the curve, the intersection of the Old Road and Bradley Lane were just visible.

"Shh!" Amy said. "Look."

Standing where a thick row of eucalpytus trees hid them from the road, three boys were in plain sight from the top of the orchard hill. They were peering out, occasionally, to see if anyone was coming up the road. It was funny—spying down on the spies, as they laid in wait. Amy couldn't help laughing; and Jason laughed, too, so noisily that it scared Amy for a minute, for fear Gordie and his friends might hear.

Two girls appeared then, walking along the road toward the crossroads. By squinting her eyes a little, Amy could see that it was Alice and Shirley—coming, no doubt, to see what happened when Gordie caught the new boy away from school. Alice and Shirley knew more—and talked more—about other people and their business than anyone else in Taylor Springs. Suddenly Amy could just imagine what they would say if they glanced up the hill and saw her there—way out in the orchard with the crazy new boy. She grabbed Jason's arm and pulled him back out of sight.

"Come on," she said. "Let's get out of here before they see us."

She didn't feel like talking after that, so they walked in silence until they reached Bradley Lane, only a short way from where Jason lived.

"Good-bye," she said. "I have to go back now all the way, because if they see me coming out of Bradley Lane they'll get suspicious. I'm going to be very late getting home, and I'll probably get in trouble."

"Thank you," he said, "for showing me the way. If you can come over on Saturday or Sunday, I'll show *you* the way somewhere."

"Where?" Amy asked quickly.

"Up there." Jason motioned toward the Hills. "Up there where the old house is—in the stony valley."

"Stone Hollow?" Amy said angrily. "Look. I don't want to go to Stone Hollow. I already know how to get there, but I'm not going to go there. Not ever. I'm not crazy."

She started home then. Back along the long-cut and all the long way home, her mind kept returning to Stone Hollow and what might, or might not, happen if she should decide to go there someday. As she walked down the Old Road, she kept looking up, over her left shoulder to where the Hills began, in a rolling tumble of foothills, piling upward into the steep slopes beyond.

After a while she began to run, and she did not stop until she reached the front gate at the Hunter farm.

chapter six

There was only the one church in Taylor Springs. There had been another once, a Catholic church, but it had burned down. Since that time a visiting priest held masses now and then in the Grange Hall for the Catholics of the valley—mostly Mexican or Basque families who worked on farms and ranches in the out-lying areas. But when most of the people of Taylor Springs spoke of church, they meant the Fairchild Community Church, an old brown shingled structure on Grant Street, not far from the center of town.

Everybody in Taylor Springs went to church. Some of them went more often than others, of course, but nearly everyone went at least now and then. Besides Grandpa Simmons, who wasn't allowed anymore be-cause he forgot where he was and talked out loud about embarrassing things, Amy knew of only two others who never went to church at all. One of them was Old Ike, Aunt Abigail's hired man, and the other was Daniel Polonski, Amy's father. Nobody knew why Old Ike didn't go to church, but Amy's father said he didn't go because he felt the Polonski family put in plenty of church hours without him wheeling himself down the aisle every Sunday. He was referring to the fact that Amy's mother went to church a lot—probably more than anyone else in the whole valley, except perhaps the Reverend Dawson himself.

On Sunday mornings Helen Polonski went to Sunday School and the worship service that followed, and then on Sunday evenings she went to the youth meeting as a sponsor and stayed on for the evening service. During the week she went to prayer meeting and Bible study and missionary sewing circle and twice to choir practice. Amy would probably have gone to everything, too, if it hadn't been for Aunt Abigail.

Abigail Hunter usually went to Sunday morning service, unless a noisy visiting revivalist was speaking, and she also went every Thursday afternoon to sew for the missionaries. But that was all. And she insisted that Sunday morning was enough time for Amy to spend in church. It was the one subject on which Amy's aunt and father agreed. Not that they would have thought of it as an agreement—but the results were the same. Aunt Abigail said, "Too much church can be as bad as too little, Helen. Remember what happened to that pious Paulsen boy." And Amy's father said, "Stay home with me, Baby. We got enough saints in the family already." But it was enough like an agreement to keep Amy from going to church as much as she might otherwise have had to.

Actually, Amy knew of one other subject on which her aunt and father agreed, and that was the town of Taylor Springs. According to Aunt Abigail, Taylor Springs was a typical backwoods town full of narrow-minded superstitions, and besides that it was a trap.

"Yes, a trap, Amy Abigail," she said. "Oh, it's fine for some people, but it's not the place for someone with energy and ability. I want you to promise me that you'll get away from here as soon as you're old enough to be on your own."

"But I like it here," Amy had said. "And besides I'll be leaving pretty soon anyway. Just as soon as Daddy gets an office job and—"

"Well, perhaps. But don't wait for that to happen. Don't wait too long, the way I did."

It was plain that Aunt Abigail felt that she had been trapped in Taylor Springs. And although Amy's father didn't talk about it, Amy knew he felt the same way. But no one else that Amy knew felt that way about Taylor Springs. Just about everyone else agreed that Taylor Springs was a great place to live. And it was also pretty much agreed upon that you

72

could tell how good a person was by the amount of time he spent in church. Sometimes Amy resolved to start going more often, but usually she only went when she had to, on Sunday mornings.

It was during church on the Sunday morning after she had met Jason Fitzmaurice that Amy made an important decision. It was not the kind of decision one might expect to make in church, involving as it did deception and disobedience and perhaps some other sins as well. And it might not have happened at all if the Reverend Dawson hadn't chosen that morning to preach one of his sermons on alcohol.

As soon as he began on the text for the day— Proverbs 23:21: "For the drunkard and the glutton shall come to poverty—" Amy knew most of what he was going to say in the next forty minutes. She knew because she had heard the Reverend's alcohol sermons many times before, although she always tried very hard not to listen to them. She had tried various ways of not listening, and had discovered that to simply concentrate on not listening didn't work at all. The best way not to listen she had found was to do what Aunt Abigail called "wool-gathering."

Wool-gathering was simply letting your mind get involved with a subject interesting and complicated enough to keep you from thinking about what you were supposed to be hearing. Amy did it quite a bit without even trying. One of her favorite subjects to wool-gather about was the Lilliputians. Since she had finished reading *Gulliver's Travels*, she had invented her own colony of Lilliputians, who lived in various places around the Hunter farm, where she could protect and care for them and rescue them from all kinds of dangers. There were five families of them and she knew all about each of them, their names and ages and special characteristics.

Thinking about the Lilliputians was usually interesting enough to hold Amy's attention no matter what the circumstances, but the Reverend Dawson's alcohol sermon made even the best wool-gathering difficult to maintain. The Reverend tended to become, not only very dramatic, but also very loud when he talked about the evils of drink, and words and phrases kept breaking through. Bits and pieces of terrible tragic stories about the victims of alcohol kept creeping through into Amy's consciousness, and along with them, as she had known it would, came the memory of a long succession of brown paper bags.

The paper bags were Old Ike's. At least he brought them. He brought one with him every Thursday afternoon when he came to visit Amy's father while her mother and aunt were away sewing for the missionaries. The paper bag always sat on the floor between Old Ike's chair and her father's wheelchair, and Ike always took it away with him when he left, but afterward Amy often had to help her father get out of his chair and onto the bed for a nap. At those times his breath smelled strange, sweet and yet bitter, and he sometimes said strange and unexpected things.

The paper bags and hellfire and eternal damnation were winning out over the Lilliputians, when the preacher happened to say something about heathens, and that was what brought about Amy's decision. The word "heathens" made Amy think of Jason, and from there she was soon thinking about Stone Hollow.

She had always known, really, that Stone Hollow was one of those things that she would eventually have to learn more about. She had tried, certainly, but only by asking questions. By asking questions she had managed to pick up many bits and pieces of information—information that varied all the way from Old Ike's curt and angry nod when she asked him if he had really helped to carry the bootleggers' bodies down from the Hollow, clear to little Bobby Parks's story about the man-eating cow. But now that it seemed certain she had learned all that was possible by asking questions, she was going to have to think about doing something more drastic—more drastic and more dangerous. And if she did something dangerous, it wouldn't be the first time.

There was, for example, the time that Alice Harris had told her something about how boys were really different from girls—besides things like having shorter hair and bigger muscles. Amy had known it wasn't wise, but because she wanted to know so badly, she had risked asking her mother about it. She hadn't really gotten into trouble that time, at least not trouble of the usual kind like punishment or scolding. But right afterward her mother had added a new part to the prayer she said with Amy every night, a part about keeping a clean mind and a pure spirit. Since then it had been hard to keep her mind on the rest of the prayer because of waiting for that part—and knowing how it would make her feel. It was strange how words like "clean" and "pure" could make you feel just the opposite. It was a feeling Amy hated almost more than a spanking. And what made it especially bad was that it was all for nothing, because she hadn't found out anything more than what she already knew.

Amy admitted to herself that morning that Stone Hollow would probably turn out to be one of the more dangerous things that she had to find out about. Dangerous, that is, if she did more than just ask questions. But, there seemed to be only one way left to find out about Stone Hollow and that was to go there. Going there had been in the back of her mind before, but going alone had seemed impossible, and she had known that none of her friends would go with her. Alice Harris, who was by far the most daring about things like that, had only been willing to go to the rim of the valley and look down. But now it was different. Now Amy knew someone who would go with her and who, as incredible as it seemed, had actually been there before.

Not that she would have chosen Jason Fitzmaurice

to go anywhere with if she'd had a choice. There would be a lot of problems. First there would be making sure, somehow, that he wouldn't tell anyone about it afterward. Amy could just imagine what the kids at school would say if they found out. Then there would be the problem of making it clear to Jason that agreeing to go to the Hollow with him didn't mean that they were friends, or that she would be willing to talk to him at school, or anywhere else where there were people around. And last, there was the fact that she would have to go without permission. Not that that was Jason's fault, or at least not entirely. She knew perfectly well that she could never get permission to go to the Hollow with anyone—but to go with a boy, and a crazy boy at that, was just one more thing to hide—and then feel guilty about.

But none of that seemed to matter, or at least not enough. Amy knew suddenly that she *was* going to go to Stone Hollow, and the thought filled her with an irresistible kind of terror. She was exploring the terror —sitting quietly in the pew next to Aunt Abigail, with her hands folded in her lap, but really caught up in a world of fearfully fascinating possibilities—when two words broke through and brought her back to reality with a terrible shock.

The words were "STONE HOLLOW," and they had been almost shouted from the pulpit by the Reverend Dawson. Amy's eyes flew open to see the preacher staring sternly in her direction. For a terrible panic-stricken moment Amy was sure that God must have told Reverend Dawson what she was considering—to punish her for what she was thinking, and for not listening to the sermon. But as she sat, stunned and horrified, the preacher's eyes turned away, and he went on speaking. His voice had sunk now to a tragic whisper, and he was saying something about "those two unfortunate sinners, whose awful deaths were just another sacrifice on the altar of Demon Rum."

Even then, it took a few moments for Amy to realize that the preacher had not been talking just to her, but had simply come to the part in his sermon where he mentioned the two bootleggers as a good example of what happened to people who drank. When she was finally sure, she felt terribly relieved and grateful. Grateful enough to force herself to put everything else out of her mind and to concentrate on what the Reverend Dawson was saying.

The last part of the sermon was about a sinner burning in hell and reaching up and begging the angels for a drop of water. Reverend Dawson always lingered over that part of the sermon, describing the sinner and what was happening to him in great detail so that you could almost see what he looked like, even if you tried not to. Amy tried not to because she was afraid he might look familiar—that he might have a thin dark face, a handsome face, except for the purple shadows that came from pain and too little sunshine.

When the sermon was finally over, Amy hoped that God had noticed that she had listened carefully to the last part of the sermon, even though it hadn't been easy. She hoped that that would do some good. She tried not to notice, so that God wouldn't, that at the very back of her mind her resolution to visit Stone Hollow with the crazy boy was still there, although she was trying to pretend that it wasn't.

chapter seven

Having made a decision, Amy liked to act on it as soon as possible. She hated waiting, and besides Sunday afternoon was almost the only time she could get away unobserved. So she decided to find Jason and get him to go with her to Stone Hollow that very afternoon. The only difficulty was that she did not know where he would be.

She had to wait until after Sunday dinner, of course, which in Taylor Springs was eaten in the middle of the day. Then she would ask permission to take Caesar for a walk, and she would start looking for Jason. After that she would just see what happened.

"Caesar really needs a walk," she told her mother when dinner was almost over. "Old Ike doesn't take him walking very often anymore. Could I take him for a nice long walk this afternoon?"

Amy's mother sighed, and the crease deepened between her eyes. "Aunt Abigail and I were planning to visit the Gerhardt sisters this afternoon. I planned on your staying home with your father."

"Let her go," Amy's father said. "I don't need a keeper." He pushed his chair back from the table and wheeled it out of the room.

Holding back another sigh with her fingers, Amy's mother watched him go. "Well, all right, dear," she said. "You may as well go. But don't be gone long, and be careful."

Amy never went anywhere without her mother's warning about being careful. She knew all the things she was supposed to be careful of by heart. When they lived in the city, the warnings had been mostly about traffic and people, but in Taylor Springs there were many other things to keep in mind. In the country, one had to be careful about such things as rattlesnakes and black widow spiders and rabid skunks and flash floods and heatstroke and poison oak—and of course people, too, even in Taylor Springs, but not as much, because there were not nearly so many strangers.

"I'll be careful," Amy promised. She jumped up from the table and began to clear off so fast that Aunt Abigail had to warn her twice about the good china. The moment the last dish was off the table, she was out the back door and running toward the barn.

She found Caesar where she thought she would, sleeping just inside the door of the hay barn. There he was, spread out on his side, flat and dead-looking, his shaggy gray hide draped saggily over his bony ribs. When he heard Amy's running feet, he lifted his head and grinned, letting his tongue escape and flop from the side of his mouth. His tail thumped twice, weakly, before he collapsed, as flat and dead as before.

"You lazy thing," Amy said. "The vultures are going to find you someday and eat you half up before they notice you're alive." She began to walk slowly around the motionless form. "Poor dead dog," she said. "Poor old dead dog. I am the fairy princess, and I am going to take pity on the poor dead dog and say the magic word. I am going to say—walk! You want to go for a *walk*, Caesar?"

As soon as he heard "walk," Caesar sprang to his feet, shedding dust and hay and, judging by appearances, about a dozen years, too. He pranced around Amy, head high, tail waving, panting in anticipation.

"Okay," Amy laughed, as he bounced against her. "Just a minute 'til we ask Old Ike if you can go."

They found the old man in the tack room mending a harness. Amy approached him quietly and waited for him to notice her and speak first. Nobody rushed Old Ike, particularly children. Amy had found that out a long time ago. He turned slowly and looked at Amy and the prancing dog, his frown deepening. Old Ike always frowned, but for special occasions, like having to talk to people, he made the frown even more impressive, by making his eyebrows come clear together over the bridge of his long, hooked nose.

"All right," he said. "Take him. Take the devil dog. He don't belong to me nohow. Don't even pretend to since my knee give out and I can't walk much no more."

He turned his back, still muttering to himself, and as Amy backed away she heard him saying "—not my dog and never was." A few steps outside the door, she turned and ran.

Passing the windows of the house, she dropped to a running walk, but once she was safely out on the Old Road, she shifted back to top speed, with Caesar running and leaping beside her. She didn't slow down again until her side began to ache and her lungs felt stretched and burny. When she neared the turnoff to Bradley Lane, she began to whistle and talk loudly to Caesar so that Jason would be sure to hear her if he were somewhere in the area.

"Come here, Caesar," she called. "Stop that. Come back here and walk with me."

Caesar, who was busy with his version of a walk, coursing back and forth across the road, investigating interesting smells, seemed to know she was only talking to make a noise. Acknowledging her commands with a wave of his tail, he went right on with his explorations. And Amy went on calling and whistling.

Of course, the obvious thing to do would be to go

to the Bradley house and knock on the door and ask for Jason, but there were a lot of reasons why that wasn't possible. For one thing, one of Jason's parents might answer the door. Amy had never met heathens before, or people who wrote books, and she felt sure she wouldn't know how to talk to them. It would be almost like trying to talk to Grandpa Simmons, who was always saying something that made so little sense there was absolutely no way to answer sensibly. The most important reason, though, was simply that girls didn't go calling on boys—it just wasn't one of the things you did in Taylor Springs.

There was no sign of Jason near the clump of eucalyptus, so she went on up the lane until she came to the first good climbing tree. She shinnied up the trunk to the first branch and then scrambled higher, stopping now and then to look around. She was about as high as she dared go when, looking down, she saw a figure coming around the bend in the lane. It was Jason all right, and he was walking fast and looking around, as if he were hunting for something or someone in particular. As Amy watched unseen in her treetop perch, Jason and Caesar saw each other at the same moment. Jason walked toward Caesar, holding out his hand. Amy couldn't hear what he was saying, but she could see that Caesar was behaving in a very unusual manner.

As a rule Caesar, who was only sedately enthusiastic even with old friends—except, of course when a walk was mentioned—was shy and sometimes even threatening with strangers. But now, as Jason approached, he cocked his head and bounded forward. Sinking down onto his belly at Jason's feet, he wagged his tail frantically and licked eagerly at the boy's hand. Jason bent over the dog, petting and talking to him for a long time before he stood up and looked around.

"Amy," he called. "Where are you?"

Amy climbed down from the tree. Still shinnying down the trunk, she yelled at Jason accusingly, "Have you been hanging around my house?"

She didn't hear any answer, and when she reached the ground and had finished brushing the tree ants and itchy pieces of bark off her arms and legs, she faced him, jutting her jaw.

"Have you?" she demanded.

"Why do you think I've been hanging around your house?" Jason asked.

"Because you knew Caesar was our dog. How'd you know I was here because Caesar was?"

Jason looked at the dog. "Caesar?" he said. "Who named him that?"

Amy shrugged. "I don't know. Old Ike, I guess. He really belongs to Old Ike, this hired man who works for my aunt. Ike used to take long walks a lot before his leg got bad. Years ago he came back from a walk in the Hills, and he had Caesar with him, and he's had him ever since. Only he always says that Caesar isn't his."

Jason nodded. "Did you want to go now?" he asked. "To the Hollow?"

Amy stared. She had been trying to think of an unembarrassing way to bring up the subject, since the last time they'd talked about it she'd said that she would never, ever go there. But now all she had to do was agree, and it would all be settled. "Yes," she said, trying to sound casual. "I've been thinking about it, and I think I would like to go there, for just a little while. Just to kind of look around."

"All right," Jason said, smiling his crazy smile. "Let's go."

As they started down the lane, Jason asked, "Why are people afraid to go there—to Stone Hollow? Why do they think it's haunted?"

"Lots of reasons. There was this family who lived there once and built the house, and they all died except the mother, and she went crazy." She told him everything she could remember ever having heard about the Italians, and even added a few facts that she hadn't exactly heard, but that just seemed likely—and particularly intriguing. Like, how the poor madwoman, when she was found wandering and raving, had said something about a curse. Then she told Jason all about the bootleggers and how they had been found dead, near where they had been building a still for making whiskey. And how they had been dead for a long time when they were found, so it was hard to tell what had killed them, but everybody made

86

guesses. Most people guessed that they had died of fright, except for a few like Aunt Abigail who thought they had killed each other, and the Reverend Dawson who thought they'd been "sacrificed on an altar."

Jason stopped and stood still. "An altar. What kind of altar?" he said.

"The altar of Demon Rum," Amy said.

"Oh." Jason started off, but then he stopped again and stayed stopped for a long time with a faraway look on his face, as Amy began to tell him about the Indians. She mentioned that some people said the Hollow had been haunted even before the Ranzonis died, and that way back in the olden days, the Indians had held ceremonies there to their heathen gods.

"What did they do there, the Indians?" Jason asked.

"I don't know," Amy said. "Dances, I guess, and sacrifices, and bowing down to graven images, all sorts of heathen things like that."

"Visions," Jason said, and his eyes looked so strange and inward that for a moment Amy wondered if he meant he was seeing one himself, but then he went on. "Some Indian tribes had sacred places where they went to see visions."

Amy shrugged. "Did they? Well, they probably did that in Stone Hollow, too. All that kind of stuff."

Just past the place where Bradley Lane started uphill, they came to the beginning of the old road that had once led to Stone Hollow. It had never been much more than a trail, and now that it was weed-grown and rock-strewn, there were many places where it was barely visible. Before very long it was so steep that conversation was a little breathless, but there were some things that still needed to be discussed.

"Look," Amy said. "You won't tell anybody about this, will you? Like at school or anyplace?"

"You don't want them to know?" Jason asked.

Amy shook her head exasperatedly. "Of course not," she said.

"Wouldn't they like it? Wouldn't they like for you to go to the Hollow?"

"They'd think it was funny because I went with you. They'd tease us."

"Why?"

"Good heavens," Amy said. "You're really hopeless. You know why. Didn't your friends in other places tease each other about boys and girls? You know, about a boy liking a girl, or something?"

But Jason only looked at her with wide, questioning eyes, as if she hadn't made it clear.

"Or didn't you have any friends?" Amy said.

"I had some friends," Jason said. "I had a very good friend in Greece."

"Well, didn't he ever tease you about girls? Like if you talked to a girl a lot in school, or something?"

"No," Jason said. "My friend didn't go to school. He was a hermit."

"A hermit. How old was he, for heaven's sake?"

"Old? I don't know exactly, but he was a very old man."

"An old man!" Amy said. "That's not—" But then she gave up. "Anyway," she said, "just don't tell anyone that we came up here together. Okay?"

"All right," Jason said. "Look, there's the place where the bridge used to be. We have to climb down the cliff here and up the other side."

The climbing became too hard then to allow for much conversation. They climbed down and up and then followed the faint indentation where the old road had narrowed and dwindled to little more than a path. It had been dug into the canyon wall above the creek, and slides and rockfalls had made it almost impassable in several places. Trees grew thick and tall in the canyon, and in several places had fallen across the road so that it was necessary to climb over a trunk or scramble through branches. Finally they came to a place where the canyon became very steep and narrow, and the road turned very steeply up toward the crest of the range of hills.

Amy remembered the spot. They were very close to the Hollow, now. From the crest just above them, you could look directly down into the narrow oval valley on the other side that was known as Stone Hollow. As they zigzagged up the face of the hill, she noticed that Caesar was not exploring smells and running in circles as he usually did. Instead he was running ahead of them, his head up and high and his ears pointed straight forward. Amy's heart was thundering as they reached the top of the hill, and she knew it was not just from the strain of climbing.

Below them the narrow canyon that had been formed by the water of Stone Hollow Creek spread out into a small valley surrounded by steep hills. At the downward side of the valley, the creek disappeared into a deep and narrow ravine, so that the valley looked like an oblong bowl marred at one end by a narrow crack. Part of the valley floor had been cleared of trees, but near the center a few huge oaks remained, and it was there that the Italian family had built their little house.

The shack stood in the deep shade of the old trees, its roof sagging crazily and its doors and windows gaping like the eyes and mouth of a frightened face. Amy had thought of that when she saw the house before— that it looked as if it were crying out in fear.

"Look," she whispered to Jason. "Even the house looks frightened."

But Jason didn't answer. He was standing stiffly, staring down into the valley, with his head slightly turned as if he were listening to something from below. Beside him, Caesar was doing the same thing, his head cocked and his ears cupped forward. Amy moved closer and, as she put her hand on Caesar's back, she could feel that he was trembling.

chapter eight

Silence. One of the first things that Amy noticed as they started down into the Hollow was the silence, a kind of quietness that made even the slightest sound echo and throb like the whistle of a train. Amy found herself listening avidly to a single faint bird call and then, as they neared the oak trees, to the occasional rasping whisper of an invisible breeze.

Ahead of her, Jason walked light and quick, looking around eagerly; and not far away, Caesar trotted purposefully, stopping now and then to listen and sniff the air. Once or twice he whined softly deep in his throat.

Hurrying, Amy caught up with Jason and grabbed his arm. "Look," she whispered. "Look at Caesar. He looks as if he's searching for something."

Jason nodded. "Or someone," he said.

They had reached the oak grove now, and just ahead of them, in the deep shade, was the old shack. Its roof and porch sagged, and its glassless windows stared out at them as blankly as the empty eyes of a skull.

Amy hung back. "Let's not go in," she said, and then as Jason glanced at her without stopping, "Did you really go inside before? I mean, have you really been in there?"

"It's all right," he said. "It's not the house."

"What do you mean? What's not the house?"

"I mean that it doesn't come from inside the house. You can feel it in there sometimes, but it comes from someplace else."

"What does?" Exasperation, mixed with fear, made her voice come out in a breathy squeak. "What are you talking about?"

The squeak was embarrassing, but it did accomplish something, because Jason stopped and really looked at her for the first time since they started down into the Hollow. "I don't know," he said. "Not really. Whatever it is that makes it different here. I don't know what it is, but I can feel it."

"Right now?" Amy asked. "Can you feel it right now?"

Jason stopped and seemed to be listening. His face tilted upward, and his strange wide eyes seemed to grow larger and flicker with points of dancing light,

like the eyes of a playful cat. After a moment he nodded. "Yes," he said. "I can feel it. Can't you?"

Amy tried, standing as he had done with her face turned up. She felt as hard as she could—and after a moment a strange prickle tingled up her back and into the roots of her hair.

"I'm not sure," she said. "But I'm frightened. I'm sure about that."

Jason took her hand and pulled. "Come on," he said. "I'll show you the house."

It had never been much more than a shack, and now, after years of emptiness, it was only a broken rotten shell. The splintery floorboards sagged and creaked with every step, and the air was heavy with the smell of dust and mildew. Just inside the gaping doorway, the cracked and broken door lay on the floor, its hinges crusted with rust.

"Look at that," Jason said, pointing.

"At what?" Amy whispered.

"At that piece of wood the hinges tore out of the wall. And the way the door is cracked there, as if something hit it hard. It looks as if someone broke it down."

"Maybe it was a storm," Amy said. "Maybe the wind broke it in."

Jason didn't answer. But he stared at the door for a long time before he pulled Amy around it and on into the room.

The main room of the house was empty, except

for a few dust-covered piles of trash. Layered over with dirt and drifted leaves, the piles of trash were anonymous lumps, except where here and there something recognizable protruded—faded and musty articles of clothing, a part of a broken chair, and a rusty coffeepot. Under ordinary circumstances, Amy would have immediately begun to explore the trash heaps, undeterred by the dust and grime and the musty smell of mouse and mold. Ordinarily the fascination of long-forgotten articles, each one possibly the key to some ancient secret, would have been enough to make her forget everything else. But nothing was ordinary in Stone Hollow and, still hanging onto Jason, she let herself be led into the second room.

The second room was smaller and completely empty, except for what appeared to be a rough handmade frame for a very small bed. A sudden realization made a shiver prickle up the back of Amy's arms and legs.

"That must be *her* bed," she whispered. "The little girl who died of the lockjaw."

Jason stared at the bed for a while before he nodded slowly. "That's why it's here," he said.

"What do you mean—why it's here?"

"Well, it's the only piece of furniture left, except for broken pieces of things. As if people came and took everything they could use, a long time ago. Except they didn't want the bed because—"

"Because she died there," Amy breathed. "Jason, I think I've seen enough. I mean, I think I'd better be starting home before my folks start worrying about me."

"Don't you want to see the other room first?" Jason asked. "There's just one more."

The last room, apparently a kitchen, was a lean-to addition with a slanting roof. It was long and narrow and ran the length of the shack at the back. Like the front room it was scattered with piles of trash, and against one wall sat the rusted remains of a wood-burning iron stove. One of its heavy iron legs was missing, so it leaned at a crazy angle. Its chimney pipe had broken loose from its vent in the ceiling and jutted forward to end in midair. Beyond it a kitchen table with two missing legs crouched in the corner like a wounded animal.

Somehow, the kitchen seemed the saddest and the most frightening of the three rooms—even worse than the bedroom with its tragic bed. Amy wasn't sure why, except that kitchens should be warm and busy and good-smelling. In her mind it was easy to see it differently, with a neatly aproned woman leaning over a floury table, and a little girl standing on a chair alongside to watch. It was easy to right the stove and fill it with glowing heat and cover its top with gleaming pots and pans. In contrast, the desolate, dirty ruin seemed almost unbearable.

"Please, Jason, let's go," she said.

But just at that moment there was a rustle of movement and the sound of footsteps in the main room of the house. Amy grabbed Jason so hard that he staggered backward. She opened her mouth to scream, but nothing came out; and before she could try again, the noises approached the door to the kitchen and came through, and it was only Caesar.

"Caesar," Amy said. "I'd forgotten all about him. Look what he's doing."

Caesar was running back and forth across the room sniffing frantically. Now and then he made a whimpering sound. He stopped at a pile of trash in the far corner of the room, smelled for a long time, and then raised his head and made a strange, drawn-out noise that sounded almost like a howl. The howl over, he turned, ran past Amy and Jason without seeming to notice them, and disappeared through the doorway. They followed after him, out through the littered front room and around the fallen door; but by the time they emerged onto the sagging front porch, he was nowhere to be seen.

"Where could he have gone?" Amy said.

"He must have gone down to the creek. He's probably running around down there in the underbrush. Let's go look for him."

Amy nodded reluctantly. She couldn't leave without Caesar, and the only way to get him back was to find him. Calling him was out of the question. To stand there and shout into the breathless silence of the Hollow would be impossible.

A slight weed-grown indentation that might once have been a well-worn path led from the back of the shack to the creek. A second path, branching off, led to some small outbuildings that Amy had not noticed before. One of them was surrounded by the remains of a wire fence and had probably been a chicken house. The other was slightly larger and might have been a toolshed or granary.

Jason turned off the path toward the larger shed. "Come here," he said. "I want to show you something."

"What is it? What's in the shed?"

"Not the shed," Jason said. "It's empty except for some old bottles and cans and a few broken barrels. Over there, that's what I wanted you to see."

They had rounded the shed, and beyond it near the trunk of one of the largest oak trees was what appeared to be part of a picket fence. It had been a very low fence, not more than two feet high and judging by the pickets that remained standing, it had enclosed a very small area.

"What do you think it was for?" Jason asked. "Some kind of animal pen?"

Amy shook her head. "A grave," she whispered. "I think it's a grave. Look. See how the ground is rounded up there in the middle?"

"I thought of that," Jason said. "But there isn't any tombstone. And besides, wouldn't it be against the law? I thought people had to be buried in real graveyards."

"I guess they do now," Amy said. "But people who lived way out in the country used to make their own graveyards, just for their own family. I've seen them before. They usually have little fences around them."

"I don't see any tombstone," Jason said.

"It might have been made of wood and just rotted away," Amy said. "Or somebody took it. Jason, don't. Don't go in there."

Jason was climbing over the fence into the tiny enclosure. Amy backed away as Jason bent over the grass-covered mound.

"Here it is," he said, "at least a part of it." He turned toward Amy, holding up a small dirt-colored slab of wood.

"Put it down," Amy said, retreating farther. "Let's go. Let's find Caesar and get out of here."

Jason followed, then, but when they returned to the path, Caesar was still nowhere in sight. They continued on the path until it ended at the stream, at a place where rocks had been piled to form a small dam, behind which the water backed up into a deep clear pool. A smooth flat rock at the edge of the pool made a perfect place to stand for dipping water. Staring at the shady pool, Amy pictured them again, the woman and little girl. This time the woman was bending down to dip water in two wooden buckets, and the little girl was hanging on to her skirt.

"Look," Jason said suddenly. "There he goes."

Amy looked in time to catch a glimpse of Caesar trotting away from them around a bend in the creek bed. They ran after him, climbing over rocks and pushing their way through low-growing bay and willow trees and clumps of heavy brush. Rounding a pile of boulders, they caught another glimpse of Caesar, not far ahead of them. Amy called to him, but he went on as if he hadn't heard.

They had reached the upper edge of the valley now, and not far ahead the hills that formed the eastern wall rose with clifflike steepness. The bed of the creek was becoming a crevice, increasingly deep and narrow as it penetrated further into the hill. After climbing through the branches of a fallen tree, they came all at once onto both Caesar and what seemed to be a dead end. Just ahead was a sheer rock wall eight or ten feet high. The water of the creek spilled over it in a slender stream and fell down into a deep rocky pool. Near the pool Caesar was sniffing around what seemed to be the remains of several broken barrels and a large mass of metal pipes and vats.

"The still," Amy whispered. "This must have been where they had the still." She caught up with Caesar and grabbed his collar. "Come on, Jason. I've got him. Let's go."

But Jason was standing near the waterfall, looking up at the face of the cliff. "Look," he said, "footholds." Only a few feet away from the falling stream of water, a series of holes in the solid rock led to the top of the cliff.

"Jason," Amy said more urgently, "come on." But even as she said it, she knew it wasn't going to do any good. Turning loose of Caesar's collar, she got ready to follow Jason up the cliff.

It wasn't easy. The holes had obviously been dug for full-grown people, and Amy had to struggle to make it from one hole to the next. When she was almost to the top she panicked, feeling certain she could never reach the next step. But then, just above her, Jason said, "I'm up. Reach up with your left hand, and I'll pull."

With Jason pulling and Amy's feet scrabbling frantically on the sheer rock face, she finally reached a point where she could fall forward on her stomach onto a flat surface. She was still lying there, breathing hard, when she heard Jason say, "It's here. This is the place."

Amy jumped to her feet.

Directly in front of her the hill was scooped out to form a shallow arched cave, a kind of natural grotto. At the back of the grotto water trickled out of the rock wall in several places and ran down into a wide shallow pool. The water flowed around a small island of rock and then narrowed into a thin stream before it reached the edge of the cliff and plunged down into the pool below.

"It's just a spring," Amy said. "There are lots of

them in the hills around here."

Jason didn't answer. He was standing very still staring into the grotto. He did not move for what seemed like a very long time. Looking in the direction that he was staring, Amy saw only water and rocks. She heard nothing but the gurgle and splash of the falls and now and then a whimper from Caesar, where he had been left at the foot of the cliff. But she felt something.

Afterward, when she tried to think about what she had felt, she discovered that there were no words with which to think about it. The closest word was *almost* —an *almost* seeing, *almost* hearing. Like the almost memory of a dream, when you waken suddenly and the dream is still there, although no single detail of it is clear.

At last Caesar barked sharply, and Jason started. He looked around as if he were just awakening in a strange place. Seeing Amy he motioned to her and began to back toward the spot where the footholds led to the level below. He went down first, climbing easily, with his quick, agile, monkeylike movements; and when Amy started down, he reached up and steadied her feet in the shallow footholds. Caesar was waiting for them near the ruined still, and this time he stayed close by as they made their way down the creek bed to the clearing. They almost ran across the flat valley floor, past the ruined house, and up the steep slope to the ridge. When they reached the ridge, they stopped for a moment to look back.

Jason was smiling. "That was it," he said. "That's where it all comes from."

"Where what comes from?" Amy asked.

"Whatever it is that makes it different down there. The thing that makes everyone afraid to go there."

Suddenly Amy was exasperated again. "What thing?" she demanded. "What did you see? All I saw was a spring in a kind of cave."

Jason turned to look at her. "You didn't see the Indians, then?" he asked.

Amy backed away, staring at him. Then she turned and began to walk toward home. It was the first time all afternoon that she had remembered he was crazy.

chapter nine

When Jason said that he had seen Indians in Stone Hollow, Amy was too horrified to say anything. She didn't know why, exactly, except that she had spent all afternoon with him just as if he were an ordinary normal person. She had even depended on him at times when she had been frightened and he had seemed less so. And then to be reminded suddenly that he was crazy—and probably a lot crazier than she had realized before! It was a shock.

On the way home she walked fast for a while, not letting him catch up with her, glancing back now and then and hurrying when he got close. But afterward, when the shock had had time to wear off, she began to feel curious again. She began to wonder just how being crazy worked. What kind of Indians did being crazy make you able to see? Did something in your head tell you you had seen Indians when you really hadn't? Or did you really see them, right down to what they were doing and wearing, perhaps like images on a movie screen? It was a fascinating thought. For a moment she found herself almost wishing that she could have seen them, too.

She stopped and looked back at Jason, who was walking slowly now, not trying anymore to catch up with her. When he noticed that she had stopped, he stopped, too, and looked at her questioningly. She looked back, not letting her face show anything, because she really wasn't sure yet just what she wanted. After a moment he smiled and hurried to catch up.

Watching him come, it occurred to Amy that being crazy was a lot different from being stupid. For instance, she couldn't imagine someone stupid, like Gordie Parks, figuring out what you were thinking almost before you knew yourself.

As soon as Jason caught up, Amy said, "Look, about those Indians, how many of them did you see?"

Jason thought for a moment. "There were three," he said. "Three there by the spring, but I think there were more not far away."

"What were they doing?" Amy asked.

"Sitting. The three that I saw for sure were just sitting on the ground with their backs to us looking at the Stone."

"The stone?" Amy asked. "What stone?"

Jason stared at her in surprise. "The Stone," he said, "in the middle of the spring. The one standing up like a pillar on the little island in the middle of the pool."

Amy didn't particularly remember noticing, but now she seemed to recall that the little island had been rather flat, except in one place where there was a large boulder, shaped almost like a tombstone, or perhaps more like a gigantic hand. She remembered a color, too, a subtle shadowed shade, like the ghostly green of Spanish moss. And there *had* been that feeling, that strange indescribable feeling of something that was almost there—almost seen and heard. A shiver started somewhere in the backs of her legs and worked its way slowly upward.

Amy found herself staring at Jason, seeing him in a new way. And wondering in the back of her mind if there was something else different about him, besides just being crazy.

On the rest of the way home, Amy asked some more questions about the Indians and about the Stone, but Jason didn't seem to want to say more about them.

When Amy asked him why the Indians were there and why they were staring at the Stone, he only shook his head slowly.

"I don't know," he said. "I'm not sure. I have to think about it."

He was still thinking, distant-eyed and silent, when their paths parted.

Amy ran all the way home, as she always did when she was feeling tense or excited. She was almost home when she tripped over Caesar and fell down hard, skinning a new place on her left knee and making a fresh wound on the right one where the last scab had been almost ready to pick off.

She limped home to a scolding for being late, and for running, and for skinning her knees again. She wouldn't have minded the scolding much but, like so many scoldings, it turned into a discussion. This time the discussion was about how important skinned knees were. Amy's father talked about how he'd always had not only skinned knees but also black eyes and all kinds of lumps, sprains, and bruises when he was a kid in Chicago, and how it had probably been good for him. Aunt Abigail talked about good breeding and deportment, not to mention the expensive pair of stockings Amy had ruined the last time she fell down on the way home from church. Amy's mother talked mostly about blood poisoning and a little boy who'd skinned his knee and the next day he'd had red lines running up and down his leg and the following day he was dead. By the time everyone was through talking, Amy was so tired she barely had time to think about Stone Hollow before she fell asleep.

She did think about it a lot, though, the next day and the days after that. At first she thought mostly about what she had told Jason about school. How he should act as if he didn't especially know her—and how he should not mention to anyone that she had gone with him to Stone Hollow.

Actually she felt fairly confident that he wouldn't talk about it. He had said he wouldn't, and even though he was crazy, she felt sure it wasn't the kind of craziness that would make him forget a promise. There was another reason, too, why she wasn't too worried about Jason's talking, and that was because there wasn't anybody at school who would talk to him. But even though she wasn't too worried, she kept an eye on him anyway.

It was during that week that Amy really began watching Jason—partly in case he started talking, but mostly because she was just very interested. The reason for that, of course, was curiosity. Knowing perfectly well it wasn't a good idea, she found herself watching Jason from behind an open book, or maneuvering to get close to him in the classroom, or even following him on the playground from a safe distance.

It wasn't really surprising that she was so curious, she decided. It was only natural to be interested in a crazy person when you hadn't known very many. However, Amy had known that Jason was crazy since the first day she met him, and it was only since Sunday that she had been so especially curious about him. Actually, it was only since that moment on Sunday when she had seen a difference in him that couldn't really be explained as simple craziness. She didn't know what that difference was, but it was something important, and she knew she had to find out more about it.

There were many ways in which she could see that Jason was different. In the classroom he either worked hard and fast, or else sat staring at nothing for long periods of time. If the teacher called on him, he often had to have the question repeated, and then didn't seem to know anything. But now and then he knew not only the answer, but also all sorts of extra facts and details, and he told about them using big or even foreign words. This seemed to really impress the teacher—and made all the kids exchange glances that meant "show-off" or even "liar."

Once, when the teacher asked about a picture in the history book, Jason raised his hand and told all about it. Miss McMillan had only wanted to know that the building in the picture was called the Parthenon, but Jason also told what goddess it had been built for, and when it was built, and the kind of columns it had, and then he started telling how much bigger it was when you saw it up close than it looked in the picture. That was when everyone in the class really started exchanging glances.

Suddenly Amy raised her hand, and if Miss McMillan had called on her right away, she would have done something terribly stupid. She would have told the whole class that he wasn't lying, and that he *had* been to Greece, and not only there but to Ireland

and. . . . But fortunately she came to her senses and took her hand down before Miss McMillan got around to calling on her.

Watching Jason on the playground turned out to be even more dangerous. That was because the playground was a dangerous place for Jason, and the danger just naturally spilled over onto anyone dumb enough to get involved. Which is exactly what Amy found herself doing.

It was Jason's own fault that he got into so much trouble—much more trouble than other new kids. More even than new kids who were also different, like the Mexican kids who didn't even speak very much American. What Jason did wrong was to act as if he didn't know he was in danger. No matter how many times he was teased or made a fool of, or even beaten up, he went right on acting as if he didn't think it would happen again. Instead of keeping very quiet and out of sight, which was the only thing to do unless you were good at defending yourself, either with words or your fists, Jason went right on acting as if everybody were his friend.

There wasn't a whole lot that Amy could do about it, but once when Shirley Anderson and some other girls were pretending to be friendly and asking questions to get Jason to say something weird, Amy strolled up and asked Shirley if she knew there was a spider in her hair. That worked fine because by the time Shirley had stopped running and swatting at her head, everyone had forgotten all about teasing Jason.

But another time Amy got her shin kicked and was very lucky to get off with just that. That time Gordie asked Jason if he wanted to play dodge ball. When Jason was dumb enough to say yes, Gordie started chasing him and bouncing a hard basketball off his head and back. Jason backed away slowly with his arms up to protect his head, and Gordie kept hitting him with the ball and yelling, "Why don't you dodge? This is dodge ball, why don't you dodge?"

When the ball bounced off the side of Jason's head and rolled near the bench where Amy was sitting, she got ready, and when Gordie dashed after it, she stuck out her foot. Gordie fell down so hard that he lay there moaning and swearing for several minutes before he got up and kicked Amy in the shins. If he'd had any idea she'd done it on purpose, he would have done a lot worse than that.

Sometimes Amy got really mad at Jason for being so dumb about stupid people like Shirley and Gordie, and for getting himself into so much trouble. But at least he didn't tell about Amy and Stone Hollow. A whole week went by, and as far as she could tell not a single person knew that she had gone to Stone Hollow with him. But then on Saturday he did something almost as bad as telling. On Saturday, Jason came to see Amy at the Hunter farm.

Fortunately Amy happened to be out in the yard at the time. She had been sent out to burn trash, and she was making a game of it, setting up little cities of boxes and cartons and watching to see how they burned, and by what route the people of the city could flee, to escape the flames. She was squatting in front of the incinerator peering in at the flames when, out of the corner of her eye, she saw Caesar running across the yard. She looked around, expecting to see a stray cat or another dog, and there was Jason coming in the gate. He was headed right for the front door, as if he intended to go right up and knock and ask for Amy. She managed to head him off just outside of the rose garden.

"What are you doing here?" she asked.

"I came to see you," Jason said, smiling his dumb gosling smile.

Even though there wasn't anybody around to hear, Amy blushed. Everybody in school teased Marjorie Evans because Bert Miller came to her house sometimes, and he, at least, had enough sense to say he'd come to see her brother, or to ask if the Evanses wanted to buy some eggs.

Amy huffed angrily and stamped her foot. "Well, you can't," she said. "So go away."

Jason didn't exactly smile, but his eyes looked as if he thought something was funny. "I can't see you?" he asked.

"I mean you can't stay," Amy said. "Come on, Caesar." She grabbed the dog's collar to keep him from following Jason, and pushed open the gate.

"All right," Jason said. "But I wanted to tell you that I'm going to bring some food tomorrow, so we won't get so hungry and tired."

"Hungry?" Amy said. "Tired? What are you talking about? I never said I was going back there again."

She hadn't said so, and until that moment she wasn't sure that she'd even considered it. But perhaps she had, because all of a sudden she nodded, tightening her lips against a burst of excitement that threatened to become a laugh.

"Maybe I could, though," she said sternly. "I'll bring some apples."

As soon as the gate closed behind Jason, Amy hurried back to the burning; but as she rounded the corner of the house, she saw Old Ike standing near the corn bin with a bucket in his hand. If he had been standing there very long, he had probably seen Amy and Jason at the front gate.

Old Ike ignored Amy as she walked past, but there was nothing significant about that. He never noticed children unless he had to. But before she got out of earshot, she heard him begin to mutter under his breath. She stopped to listen, but all she could make out were the words "devil dog" and then something that sounded a little like "Stone Hollow."

chapter ten

Because of being late the Sunday before, Amy might not have been allowed to go walking again so soon, except for a strange coincidence. It happened that that particular Sunday afternoon there was a special countywide meeting of ladies who belonged to missionary circles, and Amy's aunt and mother were both planning to go. The meeting was to be held in the town of Lambertville, almost forty miles away. With the coming and going, it would take almost all afternoon. Amy knew that she would be expected to keep her father company, but in the rush to get ready—the milk strained and bottled, the eggs gathered, and Sunday dinner ready so Amy would only have to warm it up—no one got around to saying so. No one actually mentioned that Amy was supposed to stay at home—no one had to.

After church Amy waved good-bye to her mother and Aunt Abigail as they climbed into one of the two cars that were going to Lambertville, carrying eight or nine missionary circle ladies, all with basket lunches to be eaten at the big Lambertville church's social hall. As soon as the cars were out of sight, Amy ran for home.

When she pounded up the porch stairs and banged through the front door, her father looked around and smiled and went on reading the Sunday paper. He was sitting in the bay window in the parlor with his back to Amy, and he didn't turn his wheelchair around and ask for a kiss the way he usually did when Amy came home from anywhere. She should have guessed then, perhaps, but she didn't really. It didn't occur to her until they were at the table, and she happened to lean close to her father to put a hot pad under the corn bread. Then for the first time she knew that he had had a visitor while everyone was away at church. It was at that moment she smelled it, the same sweet-sour smell that was always present after Old Ike's visits on Thursday afternoons.

For a few worried minutes Amy wondered if Ike was going to start visiting every Sunday, as well as every Thursday, but then she understood. After the Thursday visits there was always time for her father to take a long nap, while on most Sunday mornings, church was followed by Sunday dinner with the whole family together at the dining room table. This Sunday was different in a way that did not happen often, so a Sunday visit from Old Ike probably wouldn't happen again for a long time.

Amy smiled with relief and, looking up, caught her father's eye. He grinned back and winked the way he always did when she helped him out of his chair and onto his bed for his Thursday afternoon nap. The wink said that he knew that she knew, and he also knew that she would never tell. She looked away quickly and went on eating her warmed-up fried chicken and cold potato salad. The next time she looked up, her father was looking at her in a different way. The angry twist was gone from his smile, and his dark eyes looked warm and watery. When he saw her surprise, he looked away, shaking his head.

"You put me in mind of your mother sometimes. The way she was when I first came to Taylor Springs."

"Me?" Amy said. She leaned to look at her dark face with its frame of curly brown hair in the mirror above the sideboard. "Me? You mean I look like Mama?"

"Yes, you do," he said. "You didn't get her blue eyes and blond hair, but the shape of your face and hands is the same, and that dimple near your mouth."

Amy touched the dimple. "Does Mama have a dimple—" she began, but then she remembered. "Oh yes, I knew she did. I'd just forgotten. I guess she doesn't smile much—I mean, I guess it doesn't show as much anymore." Knowing it wasn't a good thing to have said, she hurried on. "But I'm not pretty like Mama. I'm not as pretty as Mama wa—is."

"Sure you are. You're going to be a real beauty if they don't slick you down and bundle you up 'til nobody could ever tell." He laughed, but just from the sound of it, without looking up, Amy knew that the angry look was back in his eyes and the corners of his mouth. Not knowing what to say, Amy ate quickly and then hurried to clear off the table and do the dishes.

She meant to ask her father if she could go for a walk. Knowing that he would probably say yes, there was no reason for her not to ask. But when she helped him out of his wheelchair onto his bed, he went immediately to sleep. She knew from experience that he would sleep for a long time without moving or waking up, so there was no one to know if she went or stayed. Not even Old Ike would know because he always took turns drinking from the bottle in the brown paper bag, and he'd most likely be asleep now, too. So there was no one at all to know that she was going, or to wonder where.

Amy put two apples in her coat pocket and got Caesar out of his dusty bed and began to run. She ran out of the yard and down the Old Road and partway up Bradley Lane before she dropped to the ground to catch her breath. She was still sitting there, gasping, when Jason appeared.

"What are we going to do today?" Amy asked as they started off. "Are we going back up to the spring?"

"To the Stone," Jason said. "Yes, I want to go back to see the Stone again."

"What is it—the Stone?" Amy asked. "You said you were going to think about it. What do you think it is?"

Jason stopped and looked at Amy, but not as if he were seeing her. His strangely wide-apart eyes seemed to be looking toward her, and on through, to something way beyond. "The Stone is where it all came from," he said. "Why the Indians came here, and all the other things happened."

Amy gave him a scornful look. "Pooh," she said. "I don't believe that. You're just making it up because it sounds mysterious and scary. Why would a plain old stone have anything to do with anything?"

"Stones have all kinds of powers," Jason said. "Other things do too, but the power of stones lasts longer and is stronger. Stones are very powerful." He looked at Amy's scornful face and smiled a quick flick of a smile. "It's even called *Stone* Hollow," he said.

Amy shrugged. "It's full of stones. The whole valley is full of those big, rough-looking boulders. Why should that one Stone be any different?"

"I don't know why," Jason said. "But it is. I think it does something to time. It's like time moves in loops, big loops that go out and back, and sometimes the loops are very near each other. And there are places, only a few places, where there is a power that makes them pull together and touch, so that they run together for a little while. It's something like that. I've heard about places like that before. I knew someone in Greece who had been to one." He smiled at Amy and then went on walking, as if he'd said something perfectly sensible and made it all very clear.

"Jason Fitzmaurice," Amy said, "that doesn't make any sense, and you know it. What do you mean, it goes together for a while? What goes together?"

"The loops of time," Jason said. "The power of the Stone draws the loops together, so for a little while it could be right now, 1938, and maybe a hundred years ago, all at the same time."

"Oh," Amy said, and for just a moment it seemed quite possible. It seemed almost sensible to believe that time could loop around so that the past could return—which could mean that the Indians Jason had seen could have been Indians who had lived in Taylor Valley a long long time ago and. . . . But then common sense came back, and Amy realized how silly it was to think there could be any truth in such a crazy idea.

"That's nonsense," she said. "You're just making that up. This is 1938, and that's the only time it is. And besides, Jason Fitzmaurice, if there are really places like that where the time runs together, how come other people don't know about them? How come you're the only one who knows about them?"

Amy put her hands on her hips and looked at Jason triumphantly.

"People do know about them," Jason said. "Lots of people. Only they call them different things. Some of them are called shrines or holy places."

"Oh," Amy said. "I know what you mean. Well, we don't believe in things like that."

"We?" Jason asked. "Who is 'we'?"

"My family, and the people who go to our church."

"How do they know that they don't believe in things like that?"

"Because our church says we don't," Amy said.

"Oh," Jason said. He nodded and went on walking, but after a moment he stopped again and said, "I don't see how that can be."

"Why not?" Amy said.

"Because believing is not something you can be told to do. Believing is something you have to find out for yourself. I don't see how other people can tell you what you believe."

"Well, they can," Amy said. "They do it all the time."

Either Jason couldn't find any way to argue about that, or else, since they'd reached the steepest part of the climb, he had no breath left for arguing. They climbed hard and fast on the zigzag trail, and in only a few minutes they had reached the crest and were looking down again into Stone Hollow. Just as he had the week before, Caesar whined and trembled and then rushed ahead of them down the steep slope. By the time they reached the valley floor, he had disappeared into the old house.

"Do you want to go in?" Jason asked.

"Okay," Amy said bravely. "Let's go in just for a minute to see if anything's changed." This time she intended to walk right in without feeling frightened, and look at everything calmly and carefully.

As they were going up the stairs to the sagging porch, Caesar rushed past them on his way out of the house. They turned to watch him sniffing his way back and forth across the weed-grown yard.

"He keeps on looking," Jason said.

"What for? What do you think he's looking for?" Jason only shook his head.

"Probably just rabbits," Amy said. "He gets all excited like that about rabbits sometimes. That's probably all it is."

They went in, then, around the fallen door, and walked through the rooms quite calmly, as Amy had planned. Except for their own faint footprints in the dustier places, they saw nothing they hadn't noticed before. They saw nothing, that is, in the large room or in the kitchen, where the broken stove and heaps of mildewed trash seemed entirely unchanged. But when they came to the tiny bedroom, they both immediately noticed something they had not seen before.

Lying on the floor near the small bed frame was what seemed at first to be a little pile of rags; but when Jason picked it up, it became apparent that it was the faded and dirty remains of a homemade rag doll.

Staring, Amy backed away until she reached the door. "Put it down, Jason. Put it down," she whispered. "It must be hers, the dead girl's."

Jason put the doll back carefully, in exactly the place it had been when he picked it up. He looked at the doll, and then at Amy, and then back at the doll again. He looked strange—tense and glittery-eyed —but it was hard to tell if he was frightened or only excited. Amy was sure about herself, however. She knew that she was frightened. "Come on," she begged, "let's go."

Jason came slowly. At the door he stopped and looked back again. "It wasn't there when we came last week," he said.

"I know," Amy said. She grabbed his sleeve and tugged him toward the outer door. He came at last, glancing backward. She went on tugging until they were out the door and down the sagging steps. Then she maneuvered to make Jason look at her—right in the eyes.

"Have you been here since last Sunday?" she asked.

"Yes," he said. "Twice. But not in the house. I didn't go in the house either time."

"Why not? What were you doing here?"

"Just looking," he said. "Just walking around and watching. I didn't go in the house at all." He said it

firmly, and his eyes didn't move down or away, though something flickered deep inside them like the fire in an opal. She just couldn't tell.

"It could have been Caesar," she said. "He ran in first. He could have pulled it out of one of the piles of trash and dropped it there."

Jason nodded. "It could have been," he said. Suddenly he grabbed Amy's arm. "Shh. Listen," he said, pulling her to a stop.

"What? What is it? I don't hear anything."

"The wind. It's doing it again. It's blowing in circles."

She saw then that it was true. Or at least it was true that the air, which had been hushed and still as they entered the valley, was now suddenly in motion. Dry grass on the hillsides bent and quivered, and the stiff prickly leaves of the oak trees scraped together with a breathy rasping sound.

"The wind's blowing," Amy said. "But what makes you think it's—"

"Come on," Jason interrupted, "we've got to hurry." And he began to run toward the creek and the path that led to the waterfall.

"Wait," Amy called, running after him. "Wait for me."

Although she hurried as fast as she could, Amy never quite caught up with Jason on the way up the creek bed. Once, scrambling over a boulder, she caught sight of him, and called again for him to wait, but he seemed not to hear. He was so intent, and in so much of a hurry, that Amy wondered if he would remember to wait and help her when she reached the cliff. She wasn't at all sure she could make it to the top by herself.

When, at last, out of breath and exhausted, she reached the waterfall, Jason was just disappearing over the top of the cliff. But before she could catch her breath enough to call to him, he had reappeared, lying on his stomach and reaching down for her hand. He turned loose, though, the moment Amy scrambled high enough to fall forward on the flat rocky ledge. By the time she had scooted forward until her legs were up too, and then scrambled to her feet, Jason had left her again. A few feet away he was moving silently and slowly through the tree ferns and willows, toward the bare rocky area directly in front of the grotto.

He stopped, then, and Amy finally caught up, but it hardly mattered, because he seemed unaware of her existence. Standing at the edge of the clear dark water of the pool, Jason was staring toward the grotto and the large dark Stone that stood like a monument in the center of the rocky island. Following his gaze, Amy stared, too.

The Stone rose straight up from the flat floor of the island like a huge thumbless hand. It varied in color, from light to dark and from gray to brown. The greenness that Amy had remembered seemed now more shadowy and uncertain, as if only a reflection of greenish light. The upper part of the Stone was creased by several deep crevices, and its entire surface was so rough and irregular that it almost seemed to be covered with carvings. Carvings that had once been elaborate and detailed but now were so faded and eroded that no single shape was distinct and certain. What once might have been shapes and figures were so blurred and vague that the slightest change of light or angle made them seem to melt and change. Green-lit, monumental in shape, and swarming with shadowy shapes, the Stone seemed so strange and awesome that Amy could not understand how, seeing it before, she had noticed and remembered so little.

The rest of the grotto was just as she remembered it. At the back of the shallow cave, the mossy rock wall seeped tiny trickles of water that fell down into the pool below and spread out on both sides of the island. Beyond the grotto, the rocky floor gave way in places to damp earth and heavy growths of fern and willow. Above the cave, and on both sides of the canyon, almost sheer rocky cliffs rose up into the eastern wall of hills. Except for the soft trickling sound of water, everything was very, very still.

Silently, Amy moved to where Jason was standing and took hold of his arm, just as he sank down to a crouching position, pulling her down beside him.

"What is it?" Amy hissed frantically. "What are you looking at?" But Jason only shook his head and went on staring in the direction of the grotto. Suddenly he leaned forward, his face tensing, and just at that moment, Amy heard a new sound. It was a rushing breathy noise, like a high wind, and almost immediately the willow trees began to bend and toss, and the fern fronds whipped wildly from side to side.

"What is it?" she begged. "What's happening?"

But Jason didn't answer. In fact he seemed not to have heard at all. He was sitting very still, though his eyes were moving rapidly, as if he were watching a great many things at once, or some one thing that was in constant motion.

"Jason," Amy grabbed his arm and shook it. "Don't do that. Don't sit there like that. It scares me."

He looked at her then, and smiling briefly and distractedly, he said, "Shh. It's all right." Then he went back to silent staring.

So there was nothing for Amy to do but stare, too. Crouching beside Jason in the clump of ferns, she watched and listened as the wind, funneling up through the narrow canyon, made hollow sobbing noises and set swarms of dark, wind-driven shadows into motion in every direction. Changing patterns of light and shadow flickered like phantom dancers under the thrashing willow trees and back into the dark recess of the grotto. A dozen times, as she watched and listened, Amy was almost sure she heard voices mingling with the wind sounds, and more than once a shadow became, for an instant, more than a shadow —a glimpse of a half-hidden face, or the split-second sensing of a disappearing figure.

Amy's thoughts, like a broken record, went in useless circles, coming back again and again to the thought that if she got out of there alive, without something terrible happening, she would never, never come back again. "Please, God," she started once, "if you get me out of here I'll—"

But then she stopped, realizing suddenly that it might be a mistake to call God's attention to her predicament, since she had brought it on herself by being deceitful and disobedient.

When, at last, something touched her shoulder, Amy's heart almost exploded in an awful thump of fear—but it was only Jason. He still looked strange, wild-eyed, and intensely excited, but at least he was really looking at Amy—and speaking to her.

"Come on," he was saying. "We'd better go now."

Silently they climbed back down the cliff and started down the narrow boulder-strewn creek bed. Partway down the canyon, Amy noticed that Caesar was with them, but she couldn't remember if he had been waiting at the waterfall or had joined them someplace along the trail. It wasn't until they were out of the creek bed and had started across the valley floor, skirting around the oak trees and the house, that she began to ask questions.

"Jason," she said, pulling at his jacket to make him

slow down and listen, "what was it? What happened? Did you see something?"

He stared at her blankly for a moment before his eyes seemed to focus and he began to look as if he knew that she was there.

"Didn't *you?*" he asked. "What did you see?"

She shook her head impatiently. "Nothing," she said. "At least not for sure. But I kept feeling as if I were going to. And sometimes I thought I did for a minute. But what did you see? What were you staring at like that?"

"It was—" he began, but then he stopped and shook his head like someone trying to wake up and clear away the dark edges of a dream. "I don't know," he said. "I'll tell you later. I—I have to think about it." He turned away and started swiftly up the slope.

Amy scrambled after him. "Jason! You come back here. You can't go off like that without telling me. I've *got* to know about it."

Jason smiled and nodded, but he didn't stop climbing and he didn't say anything more, even though Amy kept demanding that he tell her everything— right that minute—before she went a step further. They were nearly back to Bradley Lane before she remembered the apples in her coat pocket.

"Hey," she said. "I thought we were going to have a picnic."

He stopped then, finally, but only to take a small bag out of his jacket pocket and hand it to her.

"Here," he said. "You take it. I don't feel like eating right now."

And that was all he said, except just as they parted at the intersection he said again, "I'll tell you—later. The next time I see you, I'll tell you all about it."

All the way home Amy teeter-tottered between anger and curiosity. Part of the time she walked very slowly—wondering, lost in curiosity. But when she was angry she ran. And finally she remembered that it was almost time for her mother and aunt to be getting back from Lambertville, so she ran the rest of the way home.

chapter eleven

Amy had been home only a few minutes—her breathing was almost back to normal, but her cheeks were still hot and flushed—when the sound of an automobile engine announced the return of her aunt and mother from the missionary meeting. Running to the kitchen she splashed cold water on her hot face and rubbed it hard with a towel. Then, smoothing down her hair with both hands, she hurried to the parlor window. Outside the front gate, her mother and Aunt Abigail were climbing out of the Paulsens' Model A. Then Mrs. Paulsen got out, too, and, pulling the lunch basket out of Amy's mother's hands, started carrying it to the house. But, of course, she had to stop first to admire the garden.

Aunt Abigail's flower garden was looking especially

nice, with asters and pompons blooming between the bushes where a few late roses were still as beautiful as ever. Mrs. Paulsen bustled up and down the rows oohing and aahing and talking about God. Of course, Amy couldn't actually hear her from the parlor, but she could tell about the oohing and aahing by the rounded mouth and rolled-up eyes—the talking about God she only guessed because that was what Mrs. Paulsen always did.

The Paulsens were, for the most part, a very religious family. The younger Paulsen children said grace over their lunch boxes at school and got saved or sanctified every time an evangelist came to town. But some of the older children were backsliders, and Mrs. Paulsen talked about them a lot when she testified in church. Whenever Mrs. Paulsen testified, she talked about "crosses to bear"—her own and everyone else's. Next to God, Mrs. Paulsen talked more about people's crosses to bear than anything else.

Amy hoped Aunt Abigail wasn't going to ask Mrs. Paulsen to come in. Mrs. Paulsen always made her feel guilty. She felt guilty because she knew it was wrong to hate someone who was obviously such an extra-good person, but she couldn't seem to help it. She didn't like Mrs. Paulsen, and she hadn't liked her much even before she had heard one conversation with Aunt Abigail about crosses people had to bear that made it pretty plain she thought Amy's father was one.

Aunt Abigail didn't ask Mrs. Paulsen to come in, but she did look up and see Amy in the window, and motioned for her to come out.

"Come here, Amy Abigail, and help us get all this paraphernalia into the house," Aunt Abigail said, when Amy came out on the porch. Amy started for the lunch basket, but Mrs. Paulsen held on to it with one hand and put the other one on Amy's head. Amy had known it was going to happen. Mrs. Paulsen always did that to any kid who got close enough for her to reach.

"Such a blessing to know that this sweet child was here to look after her poor father this afternoon so you could get away to do God's work," Mrs. Paulsen said.

Amy's mother looked uncomfortable, but she didn't say anything. Aunt Abigail, however, took hold of Amy's shoulders and moved her out from under Mrs. Paulsen's blessing.

"There's no doubt about Amy's being a blessing, at least most of the time," she said in a very crisp tone of voice, "but to call that Lambertville gossip party God's work is stretching things just a bit, Clara."

She pushed the basket into Amy's hands and shoved her toward the house, and in a few minutes the Paulsens' Model A had turned around and chugged off down the road.

So everyone was home again, and no one even knew that Amy had been away except, of course, her father. Because she had not been there to help him back into his wheelchair, he had had to spend the whole afternoon in bed. Amy knew he must have been awake and ready to get up a long time before she got home, but he hadn't said so. Someday when no one else was around, he might ask her where she had been that afternoon, but he would never mention it to anyone else. Amy knew that. So with that worry out of the way, she was free to concentrate on Jason and Stone Hollow.

At first she tried to figure it out logically and reasonably. She went over in her mind all the things she had seen and heard *for sure*, without allowing any imagining or exaggeration. But the more she tried to think about it that way, the more difficulty she had keeping it straight. It seemed almost impossible to keep the things that had happened for sure separate from the things that might have happened or that seemed about to happen.

Finally she didn't even try. It was really much more interesting just to let it all drift through her mind, picking up all kinds of fascinating possibilities as it went along, until the whole thing grew into an unbelievably exciting and fantastical adventure. An adventure that Amy had shared with a person named Jason, who was surely something a lot more mysterious and extraordinary than just plain crazy.

During the next few days at school, Amy found herself spending even more time watching Jason and wondering about him. Compared to the way he was when they were in Stone Hollow, he seemed quite ordinary and commonplace in the classroom. Not that he wasn't strange—there were still differences in the way he talked and dressed and acted. But these were unimportant differences that could be called "crazy" and forgotten about. The differences that didn't show in the classroom were the ones that Amy had to find out more about.

For several days Amy stopped on the way home from school near the start of Bradley Lane and waited as long as she dared, but Jason never came. Finally she decided to tell him to meet her there. By watching carefully for a time when no one else was around, she finally managed a brief meeting in the hall.

"Jason," she said, "I've got to talk to you. Meet me behind the eucalyptus trees at the turnoff after school today. Okay?"

"All right," he said, smiling his quick, eager smile. "What do you want to do? I've been going—"

But Amy was already walking away. "I don't want to do anything," she said. "I won't have time. I just have to talk to you."

Although she ran most of the way, Jason was already there when she reached the clump of old trees that afternoon.

"How'd you get here so soon?" she demanded.

"I flew," Jason said, "on the back of the North Wind."

Amy put her hands on her hips and glared at him. "If you're going to start talking like that, I might as well go on home. I came here to find out some things —some true things, not just a bunch of let's pretend."

Jason stared back. He wasn't grinning, but something about his eyes made Amy wonder if he wasn't thinking about it. "What kind of things did you want to find out about?" he asked.

"What I want to know is—the *truth!*" Amy said.

Jason's eyes widened. "The truth?" he said. "I don't know. I don't know if I can tell you that."

"Why not? Why can't you tell me the truth?"

"Because I don't know it. Maybe nobody does."

"That's silly. Everybody knows what's true and what isn't, unless—" She stopped, deciding against saying, "—unless they're crazy."

"Something that one person would say is true, someone else would say wasn't," Jason said.

"Then one of them is lying."

"No," Jason said. "It's just that the truth is something you have to find out for yourself. Nobody can tell you what it is."

"But what if you can't find out for sure by yourself? What if you can't decide?"

"What's wrong with not deciding for sure?" Jason said.

"Ooh!" Amy said exasperatedly. "Jason Fitzmaurice, you're driving me crazy. I didn't come here to talk about—whatever it is we're talking about. I came here to talk about Stone Hollow and what was happening and what made you act so strange and—"

Suddenly Amy hushed and, putting her finger to her lips, she ducked back behind the largest clump of trees. Jason followed her and, when they were safely hidden, they peered out toward the sound of voices that were approaching along the Old Road. It was Alice Harris and Marybeth Paulsen. Alice and Marybeth had told Amy that morning that they were going to come over to play real soon, but she hadn't known they meant that very day.

Amy sighed. Why did they have to pick a day when there was something much more important to attend to. Amy didn't want to hurry home. For one thing, the last few times Alice and Marybeth had come over, they hadn't wanted to do anything except sit around and talk about boys. Even on a day when there was nothing better to do, Amy wasn't crazy about sitting around and talking about who Bert Miller liked and who he didn't like. But she would have to hurry home now, whether she wanted to or not, because if Alice and Marybeth got there before she did, her mother would be sure to start worrying.

"Look," she said, grabbing Jason by the arm. "I've got to go. But I've got to talk to you. You've got to meet me somewhere where we can talk."

"All right," Jason said. "Where?"

"I don't know. I can't meet you tomorrow. I promised Miss McMillan to stay after to help her clean cupboards. I'll let you know when I think of a place."

But a time and place were not easy to find. Finally, in desperation, Amy considered trying to talk to Jason at school. It might be all right, even if people saw them talking together. She had seen other people talking to Jason lately, now that everyone was a little more used to him. Jed Lewis and some of his friends had begun to let Jason eat lunch in their special place behind the backstop, and even Gordie was letting up, spreading his attention around to some of his old victims. A conversation with Jason, then, might not be quite so dangerous as it once would have been.

So she gave it a try—and immediately discovered that school was still not the place to bring up a topic like Stone Hollow with Jason Fitzmaurice. It was not the place because, once you got him started, it was too hard to get him stopped.

He was alone when Amy approached, sitting on the top step of the playground stairs; but she had no more than mentioned the words Stone Hollow when a bunch of fifth-grade girls came around the corner and started up the stairs. As the girls got nearer, Jason just went right on talking about how he'd been back to the Hollow twice since Amy had been, and how he thought they both should go again on the next Sunday. Amy tried to drown him out by loudly asking to borrow his history book; and when it became obvious that he wasn't going to take the hint, she simply walked away and left him—still talking.

After that one nerve-racking try, Amy decided she'd have to depend on a meeting at the eucalyptus grove. The grove was dangerous because it was very close to the Old Road and really wasn't large or thick enough to be a very good hiding place. But it would have to do. Not daring to take anymore chances with conversation, Amy wrote a note and, slipping into the cloakroom, she put it in Jason's lunch box.

The note worked. When Amy approached the eucalyptus grove that afternoon on her way home from school, she checked up and down the road in both directions, and then veered quickly off the road and in among the trees. He was there all right, sitting on the ground, shaking rocks and dirt out of his shoe. He was grinning, and he didn't stop grinning even after he saw Amy's frown.

"You dope," she said.

chapter twelve

Jason didn't stop grinning even after Amy called him a dope. Instead he finished fooling around with his shoes, and then stood up and scratched his head. "Dope?" he said. "What does that mean?"

"It means dumb," Amy said. "Stupid. It means it was sure dumb to go on talking about us going to Stone Hollow in front of all those girls."

"Girls?" Jason said. "I guess I didn't notice them. What did you want to see me about?"

Amy sighed. "Don't you *know?*" she said. "I've been trying to get a chance to talk to you ever since we went to the Hollow. I already told you what I wanted to know. Like, what were you staring at, up there by the Stone, when you wouldn't talk to me?"

"Oh," he said. "That. Well—" His eyes got their

strange, inward, shut-away look. "The Stone," he said after a while. He looked questioningly at Amy. "You saw it, too, didn't you? I mean, you felt the power?"

"I don't know. I'm not sure," she said. "I felt something. I felt scared, for one thing."

"Oh," Jason said suddenly, as if he'd just remembered something. "Do you know if the Ranzonis were dark? I mean, did they have dark hair and eyes?"

"I don't know," Amy said impatiently, and then, with sudden suspicion, "Why?"

"Oh, I just wondered." Jason stared thoughtfully at the ground, while all kinds of incredible ideas began to form in Amy's mind. Then he said, "Did you ever hear the name of the little girl? The one who died?"

Wordlessly, Amy shook her head.

"Do you know if it could have been Lucia?"

"I don't know. I guess it could have been. Why? What are you talking about? What do you know about them, besides what I told you?"

"About lockjaw," Jason said. "It's the same as tetanus, isn't it? Do you know what causes it?"

"Sure," Amy said. "You get it by getting germs in a place where you've hurt yourself. Especially if it's deep like when you step on a nail. I know lots more about it, too. Like what happens to you after you get it, and everything. My mother knows all about things like that. When I stepped on a nail once, she made me soak my foot for two whole days in Epsom salts, so I wouldn't get it. She told me all about it."

Jason nodded. "A cut on the foot," he said. "That's what happened to Lucia."

Amy put her hands on her hips. "Jason Fitzmaurice! What are you talking about? What have you found out about the Italians?"

Jason looked at Amy for a moment with a thoughtful deciding expression. Then he sat down on the ground. Amy craned her neck around the clump of trees to be sure no one was coming up the road before she sat down in front of him.

"Tell me!" she said firmly.

"She was just a baby," Jason said, "when the family first came to the Hollow. They were very poor, and they hadn't been here, in this country, for very long. They probably got the land in the Hollow cheap because no one else wanted it, because it was so hard to reach, and maybe for other reasons. At first they were very happy there. The father built the house and the other buildings, and dammed the creek. But then they began to be afraid."

"Afraid?" Amy asked. "Who was? What were they afraid of?"

Jason shook his head. "I'm not sure. It was the man, just the man, at first. He was looking for something. He went to the grotto all the time, and the woman didn't want him to. Then he began to dig deep holes in the ground as if he was digging for treasure."

"Why?" Amy said. "What was he looking for?"

"I'm not sure. I think he thought the Indians had buried something very valuable. But the woman was afraid all the time. She wanted to leave the Hollow, but the man wouldn't go. Then the woman went to the village. She put a shawl over her head, and she went to the village by herself, to see a priest. She left the little girl at home with her father. And while she was gone, the little girl cut her foot."

"And they didn't take her to the doctor," Amy said. "My mother told me. She said no one in Taylor Springs even knew the child was sick until after she was dead."

"Yes," Jason said. "The mother wanted to take her to the doctor, but the father wouldn't. When she was dead, the father buried her under the tree, and then he told his wife that he had not taken the little girl to the doctor because he knew it wouldn't do any good. He said he knew that she was going to die because he had seen her grave. Before she was even sick, he had seen the grave, and he had known that Lucia was going to die. And then the woman went out and walked in the Hills crying and wouldn't come back. And the man went on digging until he died, too."

While Jason talked, Amy had begun to see exactly how it must have been. The woman crying—sitting at the table in the narrow lean-to kitchen. She could see how the woman's head with its smooth dark hair rested on her arms on the table. Then the man came in and stood by the table. He had a shovel in his hands, and his face was stern and sad. He talked to the woman, and then she got up from the table and ran out of the room and into the Hills.

Amy realized that she had been staring blindly at Jason. Her eyes felt dry from not blinking. She nodded. "That's awful," she said. "That's the awfullest—" But then another idea occurred to her. "The father," she said. "What happened to him? What made him die?"

"I'm not positive," Jason said. "But I think it was the Indians. I think the Indians killed him."

"The Indians? You mean real Indians or—"

Jason thought for a while, shaking his head. "I didn't see how it could have been the Indians at first," he said. "Because when I've been there and there've been Indians, it's as if they are there—but separate. It's as if there's something between. Not a solid thing, but a movement like a current, one you wouldn't be able to cross over. It seemed as if you could be close but not touching. Not ever touching."

There was a long pause in which Amy didn't say anything. There didn't seem to be anything that she could say. Finally Jason went on.

"But it was the Indians, though, who killed him. I— I saw them."

"Saw them!" Amy stared at Jason aghast. But then a thought occurred to her. "Jason," she said, in what she hoped was a calm and reasonable voice, "how do you mean *saw*? Do you mean that you kind of pictured it in your imagination? Because, if that's what you mean—well, I do that too. All the time. I remember how, when we were in the Hollow the first time, I kind of pictured how they would look. The Italian family. I pictured the mother and the little girl in the kitchen and at the spring. It was as if I could see them just as plain as anything. Is that what you mean? Is that what you mean about *seeing*?"

"No," Jason said slowly. "I don't think so. I think it's not the same as imagining. You can imagine anywhere, and the kind of seeing that I mean only happens there—at the Stone."

"You mean the only time you've seen them, the Indians and the Italians and everything, you've been in the grotto, near the Stone?"

"Yes, only there."

Amy nodded slowly while her mind raced. "Ha!" she said finally. "Now I *know* you've been lying."

But Jason hardly seemed to react—his eyes were blurry, the way they always were when he talked about the Stone. "Lying?" he said, at last.

"Sure. Because you just got through saying all that stuff about seeing the man digging all over the Hollow, and the mother going to the village. How could you see that if you were way up by the Stone?"

"At the Stone," Jason said, "you can see things that happened in other places. When you're near the

146

Stone, you can see things that happened a long way away."

"Then how come you just see all that stuff that happened in the Hollow? How come you don't see things that happened in Los Angeles—or Timbuktu?"

"I'm not sure. But I think it has something to do with things that are near. Near the Stone, I mean. The grotto is full of Indian things, things the Indians brought there, and I've seen the Indians most of all."

"Indian things? What kinds of Indian things?"

"Little things. Beads and prayer amulets carved out of bone or stone. I've found a lot of them. And the time I saw about the Ranzonis, I brought the doll to the grotto."

"The doll? You mean you took the doll from the shack up to the grotto?"

Jason nodded. "And once I took a letter from my friend in Greece, and I saw something that happened in Greece, a long time ago."

"What?" Amy asked. "What happened in Greece?"

But before Jason could answer, the sound of voices very close by made Amy jump to her feet. Jason followed her example, and together they sidled around the clump of eucalyptus, keeping it between themselves and the voices. By peering through a curtain of long slender eucalyptus leaves, Amy saw that the voices were coming from three boys who were approaching the grove on the Old Road. The boys varied in size from small to enormous, and it was immediately evident that the biggest one was Gordie Parks.

The next biggest boy was Albert Hendricks, Gordie's best friend, if a person like Gordie could be said to have a friend. It was really more as if Gordie had given him the choice of being slave and companion—or personal punching bag, and Albert had taken the first choice. The smallest boy was Bobby Parks, Gordie's little brother and one of his favorite victims. As they approached the crossroads, it became evident that Gordie and Albert were playing a game with Bobby. The game seemed to be Keep Away, and Bobby was crying.

As Albert and Gordie walked along they were tossing something back and forth, something that Bobby obviously wanted very badly. The big boys laughed and yelled as Bobby ran back and forth, jumping and grabbing hopelessly. "Here it is. Come and get it," they kept yelling. Then, when Bobby gave up and started back toward town, sobbing and swearing, they yelled, "Come on back, Bobby. We're sorry. You can have it now." Bobby came running back, tearstained but smiling—and they went on throwing whatever it was, just like before. They disappeared around the curve with Bobby still jumping and crying.

"Boy!" Amy said when the boys were safely out of earshot. "That Gordie Parks. I'd like to—" She noticed the look on Jason's face then and stopped, intrigued out of her anger by his strange expression. More than anything else, he looked amazed, disbelieving.

"Jason," she said, "what are you thinking about?"

"Gordie—about Gordie."

"What about him?"

"He's just so—strange. I've never known anyone like Gordie before."

"You haven't? He's just an ordinary bully. Weren't there any bullies at your other schools?"

"I've never been to any other schools," Jason said.

"You haven't? How'd you get to be in sixth grade, then, and so good at history and literature and everything?"

"My parents taught me. In some of the places we've lived, I didn't speak the language well enough to go to the schools, and sometimes we weren't going to be there very long. So they just taught me."

"Oh," Amy said, "I see." She felt as if she were beginning to see a lot of things she'd never really understood before. There was one thing about Jason that she still didn't understand, however, and that she'd never gotten up her nerve to ask about; but now she decided to try it.

"You know what I don't get? About you, I mean, and Gordie? What I don't get is why you're so scared of Gordie when you're not afraid of haunted places or doing all kinds of dangerous things." She watched carefully for Jason's reaction, wondering if he was going to be hurt or angry. But he didn't seem to be either.

"I don't know," he said, thoughtfully. "Gordie is

frightened. I think that's why he scares me."

"Gordie frightened? Gordie frightened of you?" Amy laughed.

"Not of me. Of something else. Of something that's wrong with him. He knows something's missing, and he has to hurt people to be sure he's there at all."

Amy stared at Jason, wondering how he could say such really weird things and make them sound so much like the truth. "Gee, Jason," she said finally. "You are the most—"

Saying "Gee" was a mistake. "Gee," according to Amy's mother and the Reverend Dawson, meant "G.," which was short for God and just a sneaky way of swearing. Amy didn't say it very often, and when she did, she always felt a little guilty. And feeling guilty reminded her that it was getting late and she should be on her way home.

"It's late," she said. "I've got to go."

"There *were* some other things," Jason said. "Things I was going to tell you about. I've been back to the Hollow two times since you were there. There are some other things—"

Amy hesitated, terribly torn. "No," she said finally. "I'll have to run all the way as it is."

Jason smiled. "You'd run anyway," he said. "You always run, don't you?"

Amy looked at him sharply. "I *like* to run," she said defensively. "I'm a good runner. I'm the fourth fastest in the whole school."

That really interested Jason, Amy could tell. His mouth opened to ask a question, but she didn't wait to answer. Instead she whirled around and began to run toward home at top speed, her knees high and her feet pounding over crumbly macadam and dusty shoulders. She had gone only a few steps when she realized that she was hearing more footsteps than her own, and that the others were very close and getting closer. A quick glance over her shoulder confirmed the fact that Jason was running after her.

Then Amy really ran. Tucking her chin and clenching her fists, she forced herself to the very limits of her strength and skill. But Jason, running light and leggy as a half-grown colt, drew even and then, with unbelievable ease, pulled ahead. When he was several yards ahead, he turned aside and stopped. With her head high and her eyes straight ahead, Amy pounded past him and on toward the Hunter farm. She ran all the way to the front gate, while all kinds of strange ideas flowed through her mind as rapidly as the ground flowed beneath her flying feet.

chapter thirteen

Sometime during that night it began to rain, not just a sprinkle, but a long steady downpour that signaled the beginning of the fall rainy season. For several days huge gray clouds, bulging with moisture, drifted in from the west, to pile up against the Hills and drop their burden of water on the valley below. And for several mornings there was a discussion at breakfast about how Amy was going to get to school.

Amy would have liked to walk. She had a perfectly good umbrella and raincoat, and she liked walking in the rain. Her father agreed with her, saying that walking in the rain was good for healthy kids like Amy. However, her last year's rubbers were worn out and the new ones hadn't arrived yet from Sears Roebuck, and Aunt Abigail didn't think she should risk ruining perfectly good shoes. "Or pneumonia," Amy's mother said. According to Amy's mother, wearing wet shoes all day was the surest way in the world to get pneumonia. So, for several days, Amy got driven to school every morning by Old Ike in the Model T.

Amy had mixed feelings about riding to school. On the one hand, she rather welcomed the opportunity to observe the mysterious and forbidding old man at close range. Such observation was not often possible, since Old Ike made it very plain that, if there was anything he resented more than anything else, it was curiosity. But trapped there beside Amy on the front seat, and kept busy with all the pumping, choking and coaxing it took to keep the old car running, he was fair game for Amy's observations.

On the other hand, riding to school ruled out the possibility of a chance meeting with Jason along the way, and that, of course, was of much greater importance at the moment.

But no matter what Amy would have liked, the rain kept on falling for three days, and for three days Amy went on watching Old Ike out of the corner of her eye, all the way to school and back. All the way, that is, except for the few minutes it took to pass the turnoff to Bradley Lane. During those few minutes, of course, Amy was busy looking for Jason. The rain wouldn't make any difference to Jason, she was sure of that.

On the afternoon of the third day, Amy checked

the turnoff to see if Jason might be there, and then she allowed her eyes to follow the Stone Hollow trail until it disappeared from view in the tree-filled canyon. From there she followed the canyon to where it lost itself in the confusion of cliffs and ridges in the general area of Stone Hollow. She turned away, at last, as the car rattled slowly around the turn, and found Old Ike looking at her. Even more surprising, he was getting ready to say something.

"You been there," he said, "to the Hollow."

Amy stared at him, trying to guess his meaning, trying to decide if he was asking a question or making a statement of fact.

"I—I— Do you mean—" she stammered.

"It ain't no business of mine," the old man said, "but you'd best stay out of them hills—you and that wild-eyed—"

But right at that moment the Model T went into one of its convulsions, choking and sputtering until its forward motion was reduced to a series of jerking staggers. Old Ike bent over the wheel working with buttons and levers, and whatever he had to say to Amy became mixed with muttered comments to—or at least about—the old car.

"Mutter—mutter—worthless heap of junk—playing with fire, Missy—gas-eatin' mutter—mutter—mutter— bring down evil on yourself and your kinfolk—mutter —you take it from one who got good cause to know."

The car went on choking and sputtering, and when

it finally staggered its way into the driveway at the Hunter farm, Amy was still completely in the dark as to what it was Old Ike was trying to say, and just how much he really knew.

So Amy had one more thing to worry about and that was certainly something she didn't need at the moment. In the past few days she had already worried and wondered herself into a dose of camomile tea and the job of polishing the Fairchild silver tea service. Ever since the afternoon she had talked to Jason, no matter what she was doing, she would find herself coming out of a daze with someone staring at her in consternation.

"What are you thinking about, child? You've been standing in the middle of the floor drying that one plate for five minutes."

"Amy dear, you didn't hear a word I said. Is something the matter? Here, let me feel your forehead."

They had all noticed it at home, and they had all agreed that something should be done. But, as usual, they didn't agree about what it should be. Amy's mother thought she looked peaked and decided that perhaps some camomile tea would help. Aunt Abigail said she thought Amy just needed something constructive to do with her time, and climbed up on a chair and got the silver tea service down from the top shelf in the pantry. Amy's father said Amy needed to get out and have some fun, but nobody did anything about that.

Of course, Amy knew exactly what she needed, but there was no way to do anything about that until the rain stopped. In the meantime she could only try not to think about Jason and Stone Hollow except when she was all by herself. The best time was after everyone else had gone to bed.

Every night, after the rest of them had gone to their rooms, Amy wrapped herself in a warm blanket and tiptoed down the hall to the storage room. Cocooned in the heavy blanket in the cold dark room, she sat cross-legged on the steamer trunk and stared out the window at the dark, rain-blurred masses of the Hills.

There she tried to think and plan and decide. Could Jason possibly have started from what she herself had told him about the Italians and the Indians, and made up all the rest? Or, on the other hand, could there really be such a thing as a Time Stone, and was there really something about Jason that made him able to see and understand things that most other people could not see and understand?

Alone, there in the darkness, with only a thin pane of glass between herself and the storm, the ideas that came easily and naturally were as wild and dark and clouded as the night. Amy found that it was hard to keep her thoughts from flowing as freely as the dark wet wind.

During the day, however, things were quite different. During the day Amy, and Jason too, were cooped up in a stuffy schoolroom, packed so full of restless

sixth-graders that it was hard to escape the smell of wet hair and sweaters, and whispered bits of private conversations. There in the classroom, squeezed in between Shirley and Marybeth, Amy was embarrassed even to remember the wild ideas that had seemed so possible the night before. By daylight everything seemed so different, so ordinary and predictable. Everything—even Jason himself.

As a matter of fact, Amy decided, Jason was looking more ordinary all the time. He had recently started wearing long pants made of corduroy instead of the short, foreign-looking ones. His hair was shorter, and his face even seemed to have filled out a little, making his eyes seem less huge and owly. Watching him struggling with a math paper, chewing on his pencil and squirming in a perfectly normal way, Amy began to plan some very pointed questions—and even a few accusations—to be used the next time they had a chance to talk.

The fourth day began as wet as the three that came before, but the sky cleared before noontime, and by afternoon recess the schoolyard was dry enough to use. They would, however, have to stay on the blacktop, Miss McMillan announced, so it would be best if they organized a game before going out. Amy's hand shot up so quickly that she got called on first for a suggestion.

"Let's have races, Miss McMillan," Amy said. "We haven't had races for a long time." It all happened so quickly that even as she said it, Amy was not sure exactly what she had in mind and what she thought was going to happen. Maybe she only wanted to find out if Jason could really run as fast as he seemed to be running that day on the Old Road. Or maybe a very quick and sneaky part of her mind actually foresaw what was going to happen, and wanted it to.

Running was a very important accomplishment at Taylor Springs School. For instance, just because Betsey Rayburn could beat everybody but Bert Miller, and had on occasion beaten him, she had always been favored in special ways. She was not only chosen up quickly for games, but also at various times had been elected class president, secretary, Christmas party chairman, and had even been selected to be Priscilla in the Thanksgiving play. Betsey and Bert could not be persuaded to race very often, probably because they were both afraid of losing, but when they did, it was considered the most exciting sports event of the season at Taylor Springs School. So that afternoon, when the crazy new boy not only beat both Bert and Betsey, but beat them badly and consistently, it caused something of a sensation.

As Jason flew across the finish line far ahead of Bert Miller for the second time, Alice Harris stopped bouncing up and down with excitement and grabbed Amy's arm.

"Isn't that fantastic?" she said. "I just been dying to see somebody beat old stuck-up Bert Miller. I been dying to see that for a long time."

Shirley Anderson giggled, nodding in agreement. "Me too," she said. "Who would have thought that that skinny little Jason could run like that? I sure wouldn't have thought it."

"Me neither," Amy said.

Alice was looking puzzled. "You know what," she said. "What I don't get is why he lets old Gordie beat up on him all the time when he can run like that. If he'd just run, Gordie never in the world could catch him."

"I guess he didn't run because he's not a sissy," Amy said.

"But if he's not a sissy, how come he doesn't hit back?" Shirley said.

"Maybe there's some other reason," Amy said. "Maybe he doesn't hit back because—" an idea suddenly presented itself—"maybe it's because of his religion. My Aunt Abigail says his folks belong to some kind of different religion."

"I never heard of any religion like that," Shirley said. "Oh look, here he comes."

Jason had stopped talking to Miss McMillan at the finish line and was walking back toward where the girls were standing.

"Come on, Alice," Shirley said. "I want to ask Jason if he's going to the Playday at Lambertville School. I'll bet he could beat that great big Mexican kid who always beats everybody at the Playday."

Alice and Shirley hurried off to talk to Jason, and Amy went the other way. She walked back to the empty schoolroom and sat down at her desk, feeling strange, puzzled, and mixed up. One minute she felt pleased and excited over what had happened, and the next she felt—almost the opposite.

After a while she found a scrap of paper and wrote a short note. She folded and refolded the paper into a tiny square. After a while she unfolded it and, frowning, she added a large dark postscript.

"P. S." it said. "You just *better* be there!"

chapter fourteen

He was there, waiting behind the biggest clump of eucalyptus when Amy arrived at the turnoff that afternoon.

"Hi," he said, bouncing out at her as she cautiously entered the grove, looking back over her shoulder to be sure that the coast was clear. Amy jumped. Jason was grinning, and his eyes looked like they did in Stone Hollow—lit by small secret flames.

"That's not funny! It's dumb to scare people. My mother knows about this college boy whose friends played a trick to scare him and he died. He had a bad heart, and he just died right there in front of their eyes."

"Do you have a bad heart?" Jason said. He had stopped grinning, but there was something about the flickering lights in his eyes that felt a lot like teasing. Amy gave him a cold look, thinking that it was obvious that what had happened at school had made him feel pretty smarty. Ignoring his smart-alecky question she said, "I've been wanting to talk to you about when we can go back to Stone Hollow. I want to go there again. Do you?"

Jason nodded. "All right," he said. "When do you want to go?"

"I think I can go next Sunday afternoon. I think I can go then if we hurry and don't stay too long."

"All right," Jason said.

Amy stared at him, frowning. "I've been thinking about the things you said about the Italians and everything. I want to know how you saw all those things."

Jason was no longer smiling. "I saw them when I was in the grotto. I told you about it."

"I know what you told me. But what I want to know is just *how* you saw it. How did you see all that stuff in such a short time."

"I've been there many times. Besides the times we went, I've been many times by myself."

"I know," Amy said. "But what I want to know is *how* did you see it. Was it like a moving picture, or what?"

"How? Well, it's like—" Jason turned away and went over to sit against the trunk of a large tree. Even after Amy joined him he went on sitting silently for several minutes. His face had gone blank and distant as it had been in the grotto. Finally he said, "When it begins, the wind blows—the air moves and then there are things moving—"

Remembering the flow of light and shadow in the grotto, Amy nodded excitedly. "Yes, I saw that. I remember that."

"And then I see them. The first time I saw the Indians, I saw them sitting right there—in the grotto. But then I saw them other places, in the Hollow or on the Hills. And other times I saw the Italian family—and the bootleggers."

"You've seen them, too? The bootleggers?"

"Yes. Not at first, but the other day I took a box with me to the grotto, and then I saw them."

"A box?"

"Yes. An old metal cashbox with a broken lock. I found it in the shed where all the bottles were. I thought it was probably the bootleggers', so I took it with me to see what would happen. And then I saw them."

"What were they doing? Did you see what—what killed them?"

"I saw them building their still, carrying things, bottles and pipes and barrels."

"Did you see what they looked like and everything? Do their faces always stay the same? Is it like looking at real people, or do they change around like in a dream?"

"It isn't dreaming," Jason said.

"I know it isn't dreaming," Amy said. "But I still think it might be like imagining. The way I imagined the lady and the little girl in the kitchen—like I told you about."

Jason shook his head. "I see them because they are there," he said. "Because of the Stone. Because it makes other times, other loops in time come close so that—"

"I know," Amy interrupted. "I know what you told me about that. But what I want to know is, if the Stone makes time go in loops and brings people back, how come I couldn't see them?"

"I don't know," Jason said. "Unless it's because I'm more used to it—to seeing things like that. Or maybe it's because you've been taught that you can't do things like that."

"Nobody ever taught me anything about that."

"I know, but they teach you so much about what to believe and what not to believe. You're so used to being taught about things like that instead of just seeing for yourself. But I think you could see it. I think you almost—"

Amy was nodding—almost agreeing—when suddenly she stiffened. "Shh," she said, "someone's coming."

Quietly they got up and peered out at the road. Old Ike was coming slowly toward them from the direction of the farm. He walked very slowly, limping, and several yards behind him Caesar trotted back

165

and forth across the road, exploring for exciting smells among the fence posts. Amy rolled her eyes warningly at Jason, and they stood very still, hardly daring to breathe. Old Ike trudged slowly on past them; but when Caesar approached the grove, he stopped suddenly and, sniffing the air instead of the ground, came bounding toward them.

Ike was several yards further up the road before he turned around and noticed that Caesar was no longer behind him. Staring back at the grove, he raised his hand to his mouth as if he were going to call, but he never did. Instead he only stood staring directly at the clump of trees behind which Amy and Jason were hiding. After a few seconds he turned slowly and went on toward town.

"Do you think he saw us?" Jason asked.

"I don't know," Amy said. "I don't think he could have exactly seen us, but maybe he could see Caesar standing there wagging his tail."

"Well," Jason said, shrugging, "he probably wouldn't say anything even if he did see us."

But Amy was remembering something that made her feel uneasy. "I don't know," she said, "but I think he already knows something about us, and Stone Hollow. I don't know how he knows, but I think he does." And she told Jason about the conversation she had had with Old Ike on the way to school, building up the mysterious parts a little—the parts about "bringing down evil" and "someone who got good cause to know."

"He must have meant himself," she said. "I don't know how he would know, though. Unless he saw us. He used to go for long walks in the Hills a lot, but he doesn't walk much anymore."

Jason was scratching Caesar's head and staring in the direction that Old Ike had taken.

"Who is he?" Jason asked. "I mean, where did he come from?"

"I told you about him before," Amy said. "He started working at the farm a long time ago when my Uncle Luther was still alive. I guess he was a lot different then. My mother told me that she remembers when he used to wear fancy clothes and live a very bad life, with gambling and drinking and other things. She said her father used to use him sometimes in his sermons as a bad example. But then he changed, and quit doing anything, and got like he is now. My mother thinks he must be so gloomy and everything because he's repenting his sins."

"Repenting?" Jason asked. "All this time?"

"Well, he had a lot of them to repent, I guess."

Caesar pulled away then and trotted to the edge of the grove. He looked back at Amy and Jason for a moment, wagging his tail, and then he started off in the direction that Ike had taken. Every few yards he stopped and looked back again, as if reluctant to leave.

"And Caesar is his dog?" Jason asked.

Amy nodded. "I guess so. Aunt Abigail says that he just came back from a walk one day with the dog following him. And Caesar's been following him ever since. But Ike always says the dog isn't his."

Jason was looking very thoughtful. "Who does he say Caesar belongs to?"

"He doesn't say. He just says he's not his. Sometimes he calls him a devil dog."

Jason stood still for a long time after that, staring down the road where Caesar and Old Ike had long since disappeared. When Amy tried to speak to him, he seemed not to be listening. Finally, when Amy said, "Jason Fitzmaurice, will you listen to me!" he looked toward her, but the look was still hazy and unfocused.

"Aren't you going to be late?" he said. "We've been here a long time."

Amy glanced impatiently to see where the sun was over the western hills. "I know," she said. "But we haven't finished talking. I've got a lot more things to ask you about. A *lot* more."

But Jason was already beginning to move away. "Maybe you can ask me on Sunday. On Sunday when we go to Stone Hollow."

Amy nodded reluctantly because it *was* late, dangerously so. "All right," she sighed. "I'll ask you on Sunday, at Stone Hollow."

chapter fifteen

But on Sunday it rained again, and in such torrents that no one was able to go anywhere at all except, of course, to church. After church, Amy read the funnies and three chapters of *The Prince and the Pauper* by Mark Twain, and listened to Charlie McCarthy on the radio, but she found it very hard to keep her mind on any of it. She was thinking about Stone Hollow and what might be happening at that very moment if it hadn't been a rainy day.

"Well, anyway," she told herself, "we can meet again tomorrow after school and talk some more, and plan another day to go to the Hollow." But when Monday came, Amy woke up with a cough and the sniffles, and her mother put her back to bed and made her stay there for two days. So it wasn't until Wednesday afternoon that Amy and Jason met again in the eucalyptus grove.

"Next Sunday we'll go for sure," was the very first thing that Amy said when they finally met, "unless it's absolutely pouring. Okay?"

"Okay," Jason said. He looked at Amy questioningly. "Did you want to go for a particular reason? I mean, the other times we went you weren't too sure you even wanted to, and now—"

"Sure, there's a particular reason," Amy said. "I just have to find out some things—for myself—I just have to find out for sure."

"Oh." Jason nodded, frowning thoughtfully. He poked at the dirt with the toe of his new Buster Brown oxfords. Then he picked up a roll of eucalyptus bark and squinted through it at the sky. Then he turned it toward Amy's face and looked at her through the cylinder of bark. "It might be dangerous," he said, at last.

"Dangerous?" A strange tingle started at the base of Amy's skull and crept up to the top of her head. "Why? I mean, what would be dangerous about it? You never said it was dangerous before."

"I know. But I've been thinking about it, and I think I know now what makes it dangerous sometimes for some people. I think it's if the person is trying to use the power of the Stone for something for himself—if he tries to control it, or find out something for a particular reason."

"Hmm," Amy said, narrowing her eyes. "I get it. There are some things that might be dangerous for you if I found out. Like if I found out that you've been telling me a lot of lies."

Jason sighed. He sat down against the tree and started picking the roll of bark to pieces and piling the pieces up in a little mound. Amy, with her hands on her hips, just stood there watching him.

"Sit down," he said finally. "I'll try to explain."

"I couldn't understand it myself at first," he said after Amy sat down. "Remember how I told you that I thought the Indians killed the Italian man, but I didn't see how they could, because when I saw the Indians it was as if we were separated by—something. As if the time loops were running side by side, but not really touching—so I couldn't really reach them, and they couldn't reach me. Do you remember?"

Amy nodded. "I remember you said something like that."

"Well, I think I was right about that—if you are just *looking*. The Indians only came to the Hollow to look—to see visions. They weren't trying to use the Stone for something they wanted to get for themselves. So it wasn't dangerous for them. But the Italian man tried to control the power to get something, something the Indians had, and that made the time loops come together and touch. And there wasn't any separation anymore, between him and the Indians, and between whatever it was that they had and

171

he wanted. I think the same thing happened to the bootleggers, too."

"You mean that's what killed them?" Amy asked. Jason nodded.

"How?" Amy asked. "Who?"

"I'm not sure who, but I think I know how. I think they were poisoned. I think they found out about the Stone, and they were trying to use it to get something they wanted, like the Italian man had done. And someone came back who didn't want them there, in the Hollow. And whoever it was put something in the whiskey they were making, and when they tasted it they died."

"Do you think it was the Indians?" Amy asked.

"I don't think so. I guess it could have been. The Indians probably knew about poison herbs and roots. But I don't think they did it. The bootleggers, two of them, stayed in the Hollow while they worked at the still, and they were living in the little house that the Italian man had built for his family. They lived in the house, and they kept all their supplies in the barn and sheds, and maybe there were things in the shed that the Italian man had left there. Things like poison that he had used to kill rats and coyotes. Maybe the Italian man didn't like them being there in his house, and so—"

Amy nodded. She could see how it could have been. She could see poor Mr. Ranzoni, a stern angry figure, dark and ghostly, dressed in heavy cotton work clothes, the kind the Basque shepherds wore when they came into town for supplies. She could see him standing under the oak trees near the grave of his little girl. It was night and very dark, and he was looking toward the house where lights showed in the windows. She watched him move closer until he could see two men seated by a table. All around the table on the floor were bottles, dozens and dozens of bottles full of dark liquid, and on the table several that were partly empty. The two men were drinking, raising partly filled glasses as they leaned back in their chairs and—

"Jason," Amy said. "What did the bootleggers look like when you saw them?"

"Well, one of them was short, with a bald head, and there was a tall one with brown hair and a big nose, and the other one—"

"The *other* one?" Amy said. "There wasn't any *other* one. Two of them was all there were."

Jason looked at her strangely for a moment before he answered. "No," he said. "Two of them died, but there was another one who wasn't there when they drank the poison. I think that one was Old Ike."

"Old Ike?" Amy breathed.

Jason nodded. "He looked different, of course, but I'm sure it was Old Ike. I think he came to the Hollow first. He brought the other men there, and then after they moved in and built the still, he kept coming and bringing supplies until one time when he came back he found the other two dead. Then he went away and didn't come back for a long time."

Amy was staring straight ahead of her. "He wore fancy clothes when he first came, my mother said, like a city man would wear, and he had money to gamble with." She broke off and after a moment she turned to Jason. "I'll bet he came to Taylor Springs to look for a nice safe place to build a still, and that's why he went to work for my uncle. So people wouldn't wonder about what he was doing here. And when he found a good place, he sent for his friends."

She leaped to her feet, propelled by an explosion of excitement and curiosity. She just had to get home and see Old Ike. Not that she would ever in the world have the nerve to say anything to him, but she just *had* to see him—now that she knew. But then she remembered that he wouldn't be there anyway. That he and Caesar were still on their way toward town. He and Caesar—

"—and Caesar?" she said. "Was he one of them, too? Did Caesar belong to one of the bootleggers?"

But then, before Jason could answer, she began to laugh—at herself, for being so stupid.

"Boy," she said. "Am I dumb. Caesar couldn't have been living that long ago. Dogs don't live that long."

But Jason didn't laugh. "No," he said. "Caesar didn't belong to the bootleggers. I never saw a dog with the bootleggers. But Lucia had a dog."

"Lucia! The little Italian girl? That's crazy. Jason Fitzmaurice, you *know* that's crazy. That was a lot longer ago than the bootleggers. That was clear back when my mother was a very little girl. Caesar couldn't have lived all that time."

"He didn't," Jason said. "How long has Old Ike had Caesar?"

"I don't know exactly, but it must be about ten years. Aunt Abigail said that Caesar must be almost as old as I am because he's been here almost ten years, and nobody knew just how old he was when he came."

Jason nodded, but for some time he didn't say anything more. When at last he spoke, he said, "Then it was about ten years ago that Old Ike went back to the Hollow, and something made the past come too close, so that Caesar came through—and he didn't get back. So he just followed Old Ike."

Amy leaned against the tree trunk looking down the road in the direction Old Ike and Caesar had gone. Then she turned and stared in the other direction— toward the path that wound its way over the Hills and through the valleys until it came to Stone Hollow. At last she sighed and caught her breath, coming back to the eucalyptus grove and Jason, still sitting on the ground arranging little pieces of bark into a neat, rounded pile.

"Look," she said. "I'm going home now. But don't forget about Sunday. Next Sunday we're going to Stone Hollow no matter what."

chapter sixteen

At the Hunter farm that evening, Amy went through the motions of a checker game with her father, which she quickly lost, and then dinner. But afterward, if anyone had asked her to describe how the game had gone, or even what she'd eaten for dinner, she wouldn't have been able to say. With her mind so full of other things, she made foolish moves on the checkerboard, ate without tasting, and failed to notice that she was not the only one who was behaving in a somewhat peculiar manner. If she had not been so preoccupied, she might have wondered why no one seemed to notice that she was acting strangely.

After dinner Aunt Abigail excused Amy from her usual job of drying dishes. "Your mother and I will do them," she said. "We have some things to talk over."

Without even stopping to wonder what there might be to talk about that would be urgent enough to cause Aunt Abigail to change an established routine, Amy slipped outdoors into the darkening twilight. She went first to the barn.

The interior of the barn was a cavern of darkness, a warm living darkness full of the sounds and smells of living things. Cows chewed and belched, the mule stamped, and smaller things scurried and rustled along the walls. At Amy's low whistle the scurryings stopped, the mule snorted, but there was no answering growl or even the thump of a wagging tail. Caesar had not yet gone to bed.

Scouting around the barnyard, from milkshed to toolroom to granary, Amy saw no sign of either Caesar or Old Ike, and she was beginning to wonder if they had not yet returned from town, when she remembered that the cows had been in the barn. That meant Ike had let them in from the pasture to be milked and fed. So she went on looking.

The twilight had faded, the moon had not yet risen, and the shadow of the Hills lay dark and heavy on the Hunter farm, when Amy rounded the corner of the barn and came suddenly upon a frightening scene. A flame flickering in a mound of darkness revealed first a shadow-distorted face and then a hunched figure. Amy almost screamed in terror before she realized what it was. The flame grew, the figure straightened and lengthened, and it became apparent that she had turned the corner just as Old Ike stooped to set fire to a pile of dead leaves and tree cuttings. Peering around the corner of the barn, she watched as the old man poked the fire with a pitchfork and then stepped back. A few feet behind him, the light from the growing fire revealed, near the ground, a pair of glowing eyes. Lying with his chin on his paws, Caesar was, as usual, observing his master from a safe distance.

It was only Old Ike tending a bonfire of trash and cuttings—after nightfall so that the dew would extinguish flying sparks and the darkness make them easier to spot. Amy had seen him do it before. But somehow the reasonable explanation wasn't enough to make the scene in front of her seem reasonable and unfrightening.

Leaning on his pitchfork, the old man stared down into the flames, his thin body bent forward, his face hideously distorted by the flickering red light of the fire. Even old Caesar seemed transformed, his shape lean and wolfish, and his eyes growing redder and more fiery as the bonfire burned higher. If Amy had had any idea of questioning Old Ike about what Jason had said, if she had, even for a moment, thought of asking him if he had ever been a bootlegger, the idea was gone. Gone as completely and as irretrievably as the first wisp of smoke from the roaring bonfire. Slipping back around the corner, she ran toward the light that spilled in warm yellow rectangles from the windows of the farmhouse.

A moment later Amy burst into the bright com-

forting warmth of her aunt's kitchen, and immediately found herself in the midst of a scene as mysterious as the one she had just left, and only a little less frightening. Beside his empty wheelchair, her father was actually standing, propped against the kitchen wall and supported by Amy's mother. He was talking on the telephone. It was the first time Amy had seen her father use the telephone since they had come to Taylor Springs. The only phone in Aunt Abigail's house was an old-fashioned one. A shiny wooden box equipped with a mouthpiece and crank, it was attached to the kitchen wall at a height that made it impossible to reach from a wheelchair—and there had never been anyone in Taylor Springs with whom her father wanted to talk.

"Yes, yes," her father was saying. "Can you speak louder? I can't hear you. They what?"

"Who is it?" Amy asked Aunt Abigail, who was standing in the doorway. "Who is Daddy talking to?"

"Shh!" her aunt said sharply. "Long distance."

"Could you repeat that, Mr. Scanlon?" her father was saying. "No, I heard. My God! I just can't believe it. I start when? With pay? Mr. Scanlon, I just don't know how to thank you. Thank you, Mr. Scanlon. Thanks a million. Yes, yes. I will. I sure will. Yes, good-bye. And Mr. Scanlon, thanks!"

Hanging up the phone, he pushed himself recklessly away from the wall and dropped with a thud into his wheelchair, while Amy's mother tried desperately to keep him from falling. The chair rocked, almost tipping over backward as Daniel Polonski grabbed his wife and pulled her off her feet and into the chair on top of him.

"Whoopee!" he yelled. "He did it! That son of a gun did it."

"Daddy," Amy said, "what is it? What's happened?" But no one seemed to hear. Sitting in the wheelchair, with their arms around each other, Amy's parents were staring at each other as if they had suddenly been stricken deaf and dumb. Then Amy felt hands on her shoulders, and looking back she saw Aunt Abigail standing behind her.

"Well, Amy Abigail," she said in a peculiar voice— briskly cheerful, and yet with a strange shakiness underneath—"well, my dear, I guess I needn't have worried about your being trapped in Taylor Springs. It seems you'll be leaving us very soon."

"Leaving?" Amy gasped. "Leaving Taylor Springs? When, Aunt Abigail? When?"

"I don't know," Aunt Abigail said, nodding toward Amy's father. "You heard as much as I did. But soon, I should think. Quite soon."

It turned out to be only too true. When Amy's father finally took the time to explain, Amy discovered what had happened—and what had been happening for some time without her knowing anything about it.

It seemed that a few weeks before, the old lawyer who had represented her father's union had retired, and a new young energetic one had taken his place. Hearing about Daniel Polonski's case, he had decided to reopen it; and that very morning a letter had arrived at the Hunter farm saying that there was to be a meeting that afternoon at which it would all be decided. It might go either way, the letter said. The company might accept its responsibility for the injury that had crippled Daniel Polonski, or it might refuse to do anything, as it had before.

"We decided not to say anything to you until we knew how it turned out," Amy's father told her.

Feeling strangely numb, Amy said, "But—but how did it turn out? I mean, I know you won. I just wondered when—when do we have to—I mean, when are we going to leave?"

"Right away," her father said. "I'm to start training—with pay, mind you—next week. For a job in the main supply office in the city. So we'll be leaving this weekend." He turned to Amy's mother. "Think we can be ready in time to catch the Saturday morning milk train out of Lambertville?"

"I—I think so," Amy's mother said. "I think we could be ready by then."

"But we can't all leave right away, can we?" Amy asked. "I mean, we'll have to find a house or apartment first, and pack all our stuff and things like that. That will take a long time, won't it?"

"No," her mother said. "If your father starts work next week, he'll need us there. We'll just have to stay in a hotel for a few days while you and I house-hunt; and when we find a place, Aunt Abigail can have our things sent out."

"But—but school?" Amy said.

"You can go to school tomorrow to pick up your things and say good-bye, but on Friday you might as well stay home and help pack. We'll have to work fast to be ready by Saturday morning."

The talk went on, and Amy heard it, but somehow none of it really reached her. None of it managed to be more than sounds, sounds without meanings, that fluttered senselessly around the outside of her consciousness. Inside, there was room for only a few words that kept repeating themselves over and over.

"We can get nearly everything crated before we go"—her father's voice—"and you can get George Rayburn to take it to the express station in his truck. Find out how much he'll take, and I'll send money to cover it."

And then Aunt Abigail's—"No need. George won't take any pay. Country people don't charge for helping their neighbors."

Then Amy's mother said, "Abigail, I've been thinking—why don't you sell the farm now? I know how you've wanted to get away, and how long you've sacrificed for other people. All those years when Luther was ill, and then the last two years for us. Why don't you do what you've always wanted. It would be so nice to have you closer to us in San Francisco."

"No. No, I couldn't. That is, not right away at least. I—I've as good as promised to be on the school board next year and—there's the church—I just don't see how I could leave—just now, at least."

It was about then that Amy realized the words that had been repeating themselves in her head had somehow broken through into sound—and she had said them out loud. "But I can't go before Sunday. I just can't!"

"Why not, dear?" her mother asked. "Why can't you leave before Sunday?"

"Because—" Amy's mind felt frozen, stiff and useless. She stuttered, groping for an idea. "—because— won't we have to say good-bye to everyone—to the Reverend Dawson and all the people at the church?"

"I'll call the Reverend and explain. And he and Aunt Abigail can say good-bye for us. I'm sure everyone will understand."

"What's the matter, Baby?" her father said, holding out his hand to her. "Aren't you glad your poor old father's going to be of some use in the world again? Aren't you glad we're going to be able to pay our own way again?"

"I'm glad about the job, Daddy," Amy said quickly. But then, because she could still feel the stiffness in her voice and face, she said it again. It came out louder, but otherwise not much different. "I'm really glad about that!"

She took her father's hand and let herself be pulled

toward him for a kiss. But her lips felt stiff, too, against his prickly cheek, and she pulled away as quickly as possible. As soon as she could get away, she ran up the stairs to her room.

That night in bed, Amy lay awake for a long time staring into cold bright moonlight, and thinking the same useless thoughts over and over. Why did it have to happen right now? Why did they have to leave before Sunday, the one Sunday when she was going to find out for sure and certain about Jason and Stone Hollow? Because she would have found out for sure. There was no doubt about that. Even if she saw nothing new in the Hollow, there would have been other ways to find out what she had to know. If she could just have had Jason all by himself for another afternoon, she surely would have been able to find out about him.

She was certain she could have made him tell her the truth about himself and the Stone and the Hollow.

chapter seventeen

At school the next morning Amy told Miss McMillan that she was leaving, and Miss McMillan announced it to the whole class. During the morning recess nearly the whole sixth grade gathered around Amy on the playground and talked about it. At least the girls gathered around and talked, the boys stood a little farther off and mostly listened.

All of the girls said things about how much they would miss Amy, and some of them asked her to write to them. Alice Harris, looking very sad and dramatic, said she wondered if they'd ever see each other again—and after looked quickly over her shoulder to see if Bert Miller had been listening. Then a lot of the other girls got started saying the same kind of thing, and finally Marybeth Paulsen rolled her eyes up, the way she always did when she got to lead the prayer in Sunday School, and recited a whole poem. It was an autograph-book poem with a lot of rhymes like "roam" and "home," and the last line was about "old friends and true."

But during all of it, even the poem, Amy had trouble keeping her mind on what people were saying, because she was so busy thinking about something else. Early that morning she had decided she needed a plan, and ever since, at least half of her mind had been busy working out the details. The plan she wanted was one that would get Jason to meet her after school and, much more important and difficult, make him tell her the absolute truth about everything before she went away.

All day long Amy went over and over in her mind all the ways she had ever heard of to get people to tell the truth. She was surprised, actually, to realize how many different ways there were, but unfortunately a lot of them were not the kinds of things that would work with Jason. There was no use just asking, for instance, because she had already tried that and it didn't work. And it probably would do no good to quote the Bible or threaten him with going to hell, as the Sunday School teacher did when someone stole the collection, since it was quite likely that neither Buddhists nor atheists believed that people got sent to hell for telling lies. And as for torture—even if she believed in torturing people, there was the fact that

Jason was just about as big as she was, and maybe a little bit stronger.

By the end of the day, she had narrowed it down to a few possibilities. She would begin by trying to shame him into telling the truth, and if that didn't work she would try to trick him into it. She was still planning possible tricks when that long, last Thursday at Taylor Springs School finally came to an end.

Jason would meet her at the eucalyptus grove, that much was settled. Amy had managed a brief noon-hour meeting with him in the cloakroom, and he had promised to be there.

"I was going to ask you," he had said eagerly, smiling his gosling smile. "I was going to tell you that I had to see you because—"

"Shh!" Amy said, as footsteps approached the cloakroom. "Wait for me. I might be a little late." And she had hurried away.

As it turned out, she *was* late—more than a little. With all her personal belongings to gather and pack, and with lots of last-minute good-byes to be said, it was past four o'clock when she ran down the worn wooden steps of the schoolhouse for the last time. Without even taking the time to look back, she started off down the Old Road as fast as she could go. Clutching an armload of books and papers with one hand, and carrying in the other hand a huge paper bag containing, among other things, a pencil box, a tobacco can full of broken crayons, a clay elephant, and a half-finished shoe-box peep show illustrating a scene from *The Water-Babies*, she jogged down the road wondering if Jason would still be waiting for her in the eucalyptus grove.

He has to be there, she told herself. He just has to. And she jogged faster, clenching her teeth and concentrating on willing him to be there—willing him to wait just a little longer.

She arrived at the grove breathless and with aching arms, and for one terrible moment she was sure that he had gone. At first glance the grove appeared to be empty but, as she let her heavy load of belongings slide from her arms, she noticed a pair of legs sticking out from behind one of the largest trees. And there he was. Sitting against the tree trunk on the soft, bark-cushioned earth, he had apparently gone sound asleep.

"Jason," she said, but it came out soundlessly, either because she was breathless or because she didn't want to wake him up. Better not to, yet. Not for a moment, until she caught her breath and decided for sure just what she was going to do. Moving quietly, she circled the clump of trees until she was standing right in front of him and only a few feet away.

He went on sleeping. His lips were slightly open, and his eyes were tightly closed, so that his eyelashes made fringy shadows on his cheeks. Bending closer, Amy noticed for the first time a spatter of freckles across his nose and cheeks. He looked different with his eyes closed, not like himself at all. His corduroy pants were torn on one knee, his new shoes were already scuffed and dusty, and his hand, lying in his lap, held a half-eaten apple. He'd probably swiped it on his way through Paulsens' orchard. All the kids in Taylor Springs swiped apples on their way through Paulsens' orchard.

Suddenly a feeling of anxiety gripped her, and she reached out and shook his shoulders.

"Jason?" she said. "Jason? Are you—?"

She didn't finish the question. She didn't know, really, what it was going to be, but when Jason's eyes opened, she knew it was answered, and she found herself smiling with relief. His eyes were the same as ever—as strange as ever. Strangely set and shaded, they very plainly did not look—or see—the same as the eyes of ordinary people.

"Hello," he said, wide awake and up in an instant like an animal. "Do you have to go away? Couldn't you stay with your aunt?"

"No," Amy said. "I have to go."

He nodded slowly. "Did you want to ask me something about—?"

"No," Amy said quickly—surprisingly. Surprising to Jason, she knew, and even to Amy, herself. "N-no," she said again, stammering. "I mean I did—but I don't now, because I already know—I think."

"What? What do you know?"

"That you weren't just lying to me about—everything."

"No," Jason said. "I wasn't."

"I know it," Amy said. "So I guess I just want to tell you good-bye."

"Yes," he said, "good-bye."

After that they stood there, facing each other a while, without saying anything. It was very quiet in the eucalyptus grove, and there was a strange kind of calm, so that it seemed all right not to say anything for a long time. As if words just weren't needed.

Then Amy gathered up her belongings and started off, but Jason ran after her and put something in her hand where it was curled around the stack of books and papers.

"What is it?" she asked, trying to see over the top of the books.

"It's from the grotto," Jason said. "I found it there. I think it's a piece of the Stone."

"Oh," she said. "Thank you."

Then they said good-bye again, and Amy left the grove and started down the Old Road toward the Hunter farm. The air was very still, without the slightest whisper of wind. Amy walked very slowly, and the listening stillness was still there so that she walked all the way home without thinking or planning, and without even wondering why she had changed her mind about making Jason tell the truth.

When she arrived at the farm, she found everything in an uproar. Everyone was terribly busy. Neighbors were dropping in with good-bye gifts, and there seemed to be a hundred things to do with very little time to do them in. Caught up helplessly in the surrounding bustle, Amy had not a single minute to herself until she crawled into bed late that night.

A full moon had just risen above the crest of the Hills, and its cold bright light shone directly into Amy's face. It was just as well, since she intended to be awake for a long time. There were so many things that she wanted to think about before she went to sleep—so many questions she wanted to ask herself. Questions, for instance, about what had happened that afternoon in the eucalyptus grove.

Why had she changed her mind about making Jason tell the truth? Why, after spending so much time planning ways to shame or trick him into admitting that he had lied, had she suddenly changed her mind and not even tried? There was no answer really, except that she suddenly hadn't wanted to. She didn't know why, but all at once she had known that there was no way to prove Jason was a liar—and she didn't even want to try.

But other things she still wanted to know about. Like, for instance, Old Ike and Caesar and Stone Hollow. Now, perhaps, she would never know. There was no way left to find out.

But then, suddenly, Amy sat straight up in bed. She thought for a moment, and then slid out from under the covers and tiptoed across the room. On the floor near the closet door was the bag of things she had brought home from school that afternoon. She lifted out the peep show and the can of crayons before she found what she was looking for—a piece of stone. Rough-surfaced and heavy, it was a little longer than the palm of her hand and about half as wide. Carrying the stone and a quilt from her bed, Amy made her way noiselessly out the door and down the hall to the storeroom.

The moon hung low over the Hills, and its softly brilliant light slanted directly in through the long narrow windows of the storeroom. Just inside the door, Amy stopped, feeling for a moment confused and almost startled. The room seemed so different by moonlight. Familiar objects glowed with unnatural brilliance, or sank into unaccustomed shadow. The desk was there and the highboy and the rocking chair, but they seemed to have been transformed by the moonlight into mysterious objects, distant and unfamiliar. Amy moved across the room with cautious care, holding her breath until she reached the other side and climbed up onto the steamer trunk. But then she forgot about the room and what lay behind her.

Outside the windows, the Hills loomed against the sky, a solid dark wall except where, here and there, the moonlight touched a crest or ridge. The valleys were still wells of darkness. Until the moon climbed higher, it would be very dark in the Hollow.

She arranged herself carefully on the steamer trunk, crossing her legs Indian-fashion and wrapping the quilt around her shoulders so that it formed a protective tent. Inside the tent her two hands lay cupped in her lap—holding the piece of Stone that Jason had given her when he said good-bye. It lay warm and heavy in her palm, her curling fingers gripping its rough surface. Staring up at the dark hillside, she concentrated, forcing her mind to shut out everything but the Hollow and the Stone.

Time passed. The moon rose higher and its golden light spread down the face of the Hills. As Amy watched, blurs of darkness turned into trees and smooth dark shadows into golden meadows. But that was all. Except for a white owl, drifting down from the Hills on silent wings, nothing moved, and not a single sound disturbed the utter quiet of the night.

Amy sighed. It was cold in the storeroom, and the lid of the steamer trunk was very hard. She shifted her position, resting her head against the window frame. Leaning back against the window, she forgot for a moment about concentrating. For only a minute she allowed herself to think about the warm bed and soft pillow waiting for her in her own room. She sighed again—and in that very instant, she was aware of movement in the room behind her.

She sat still, absolutely motionless, and listened, waiting for silence behind her to prove that she had only been imagining. But instead of silence she heard the sound again, and this time she knew it was the sound of footsteps. Very slowly she turned around

and saw a man, standing in the doorway.

He was very tall. He was wearing a long dark coat, and the lower part of his face was completely covered by a long dark beard. Above the beard, his eyes gleamed, pale and cold.

Amy would have screamed in terror, but her throat seemed to be paralyzed. She shrank back against the window in helpless fear, as only gradually did she begin to realize the man in the doorway was unaware of her presence. He was looking across the room—at someone else.

The room was not the same. The trunks and boxes were gone, and there was a patterned rug on the floor. In fact Amy was not even sure it was the room she thought she was in, the storeroom at Hunter farm. But the little carved desk was there. It stood against the far wall beneath a glowing lamp, and in front of it a woman was sitting, writing something on a piece of paper. She was wearing a long white dress with a high collar, and her blond hair was piled high on her small head. Her face was very beautiful and sad.

The man moved then. He came out of the doorway and crossed the room in long firm strides. The woman shrank away from him, and there was fear in her face. He took the letter away from her and read it, and as he read, the frown on his face darkened. Then he tore it into little pieces and crushed them in his hand. The woman put her head down on the desk, hiding her face in her arms.

Two more people appeared suddenly in the doorway, two little girls dressed in ruffled dresses with wide sashes. Their hair was in long curls, and each had a huge bow ribbon in her hair.

The one with blond hair smiled when she saw the man and ran toward him, holding out her arms. He bent toward her and suddenly his face seemed quite different, as if he were not the same person at all. Smiling, he lifted the little girl into his arms and walked with her through the doorway and disappeared. Then Amy looked for the other girl, the dark one, and saw that she was standing near the desk where the woman still sat with her head in her arms. She was holding out her arms to the woman without touching her. When the girl turned and looked toward the doorway where the man had gone, her face was twisted as if with hate or anger.

Suddenly Amy found that she was catching her breath desperately, as if she had not breathed for a long time and was about to suffocate. Everything went blurry, and for a moment she put her hands up over her eyes. When she took them away, the lamp was gone and the storeroom was lit only by moonlight. Moonlight that gleamed on familiar objects—trunks and boxes, desk and chair and highboy. The room was deserted, once again only a storage place for old forgotten things.

chapter eighteen

Amy sat very still, minute after minute, waiting and watching, but nothing moved or changed. In the hushed frozen quiet, even her mind seemed paralyzed, unable to explain or even question. When something finally came to life, it was only her lips, as if they had come unfrozen first, before thought or reason.

"What was it?" she whispered, and then shrank back against the window, frightened by the sound of her own voice. She had not been afraid until then, at least, not after the first moment. After that she had been too busy watching—as if no part of her existed except the watching part, with nothing remaining to be afraid for, or with. But now, as she came back to herself, she was first very much afraid, and then, as the minutes passed, more and more curious.

"What was it?" she said again. "What was happening?" The longer she thought about it, the more questions presented themselves, demanding more and more insistently to be answered. Why did he look so angry? What made her so sad? Why did the little girls act so strangely? And then, again, *What was happening?* At last, jutting her jaw, Amy came to a decision.

The Stone was lying on the trunk top where it had slid when it slipped out of her fear-stiffened fingers. Picking it up, Amy held it—gingerly at first, and then with more firmness and determination. "I have to find out—for sure," she told herself. With the Stone clutched tightly in both hands, she concentrated on one thing—one particular question.

The air changed first. There was a feeling of movement, a rush of something like sound, except that the hearing of it came from deep inside and had nothing to do with ears.

The deep sound echoed and throbbed, the air moved, and then suddenly the man was back, standing in the doorway. The room glowed again with old lamplight, reflecting in the man's deep-set eyes, as his head turned from side to side. He looked first toward the desk that sat, where it had before, against the far wall, beneath the lamp. But the small carved chair was empty now. The woman was not there.

The man frowned and turned away. His eyes moved, searching the other side of the room where the light was dimmer, and unfamiliar pieces of furniture, some chairs, a table and an old-fashioned divan, made vague and shadowy shapes in the pale lamplight. Amy looked, too, trying to see what he might be looking for.

But then his eyes moved again, turning now toward the opposite side of the room, toward the spot where Amy was sitting, and suddenly the silent sound was moving again, more strongly, and now it sounded like a warning.

The man's eyes changed when he saw her and he smiled, but somehow the smile was much more frightening than the frown had been before. Terror-stricken, Amy watched him start toward her, crossing the room with long firm strides. Dropping the Stone, she leaped down from the steamer trunk, and ran. Almost immediately, before she had gone more than a few steps, her foot struck something hard, and she fell.

Amy fell into blackness and silence. Lying on the hard floor, she wrapped her arms around her head and waited for the unthinkable terror of the man's hand on her shoulder or his voice in her ear. But moments passed, and nothing happened. When, at last, she raised her head, she found she was lying in the narrow aisle between boxes and trunks, and the moonlight was streaming in over the familiar orderly confusion of the storeroom. The man was gone. Stumbling to her feet, Amy ran out the door and down the hall to her room.

Back in her own bed, Amy lay flat on her back, with both hands clutching the tops of the blankets, and stared up at the ceiling. Her mind raced, thoughts and ideas coming up out of nowhere, bubbling, swelling, combining and breaking apart.

She knew, of course, who they were—the people in the storeroom. Somehow she felt certain that she would have known who they were even if she had not seen their pictures so many times in the old albums. The man was the Reverend Fairchild, her grandfather, the woman was her grandmother, and the two little girls were her mother and Aunt Abigail. That much was certain. But how had she seen them—and why? She had gone to the storeroom with the piece of the Stone, hoping to find out something more about Stone Hollow, and instead she had seen them— the Fairchilds.

It was then that she remembered something that Jason had said about the Stone—that what it brought back was affected by the things that were near— things like the Indian beads, the old doll that had belonged to Lucia, and the metal cashbox. And the storeroom, of course, was full of things that had belonged to the Fairchilds. But that didn't explain their strange behavior—or what had happened, almost happened, when the Reverend Fairchild had looked right at Amy and had started toward her across the room.

Shrinking down farther in the bed, Amy pulled up

the covers until only her eyes peered out above them. Although the moon had moved higher in the sky, and its beams no longer shone directly in through the windows, the room was still full of soft shadowed light. Only Amy's eyes moved, searching every corner over and over, while in the back of her mind a word pulsed—"dangerous," it said. "It might be dangerous."

Jason had said that it might be dangerous to—to try to control the power of the Stone for your own purposes. Had she done that? Had she done that when she had grasped the Stone and—

The Stone! It wasn't until that moment that Amy realized she had left it in the storeroom. She would have to go back, she told herself, and get the Stone. She would have to go back into the storeroom. She would have to go *now*, before morning.

Amy went on lying flat on her back with the covers pulled up to her eyes. She would get up soon and go back for the Stone—as soon as she had a little more time to think about it, and to get up her courage. She would go very quickly and quietly, and in just a minute she would be back safely in her own bed. She was still planning to go, waiting for just the right moment, when her eyes began to feel warm and heavy. She let them close, only for an instant, to rest them—and when she opened them again, the light streaming in through the windows came from a bright morning sun. The clock on the bedside table said eight-thirty. Amy leaped out of bed, staggering a little from sleepiness and started down the hall. She was almost to the door of the storeroom before she realized that it was open, and that there were voices coming from inside the room.

Fully awake in an instant, Amy tiptoed cautiously to the door and peeked around it into the room, expecting to see almost anything. But all she saw was her mother and Aunt Abigail taking old clothes and linens out of the steamer trunk and putting them in boxes.

"Amy," her mother said, "what are you doing peeping around the corner like that?" She smiled as Amy came out from behind the door. "Are you awake or sleepwalking?" she asked. "Just look at yourself." She pointed to the mirror over the rosewood dresser, and Amy looked, catching a glimpse of tousled hair, flushed cheeks and a rumpled nightgown.

"What are you doing?" Amy said. "What are you *doing*?"

Amy's dismay must have sounded in her voice because both her mother and aunt stopped working and turned to look at her.

"We're cleaning out this old trunk," Aunt Abigail said, "so your mother can use it for your trip."

"Isn't it nice of Aunt Abigail to let us use her trunk?" Amy's mother said. "See what a nice one it is with all these drawers and a place for hanging clothes, like a little closet. It'll come in so handy until we get settled down in a permanent place."

"Might as well serve a useful purpose," Aunt Abigail said. "Never's been used for anything except for storage space." She turned to Amy. "I bought this trunk with the first money I ever earned. Right after I got out of school. Had some romantic notion about getting away on a long trip, but it just never happened. Then when Luther and I got married, I thought we might use it someday for our honeymoon, but we never were able to get away. Been sitting right here in this very room for over thirty years. Might as well be used for its intended purpose, for once."

"Abigail," Amy's mother said, "I *do* wish you'd think about getting away, too. Perhaps if you only came to the city on a visit first, to see how you like it. Perhaps—"

"Amy Abigail," Aunt Abigail interrupted, "what are you doing down there? Did you drop something?"

Amy had been down on her knees looking under the dresser and highboy. "No," she said. "No, I didn't drop anything. Not just now I didn't. Did you see—" She stopped, realizing that there would be no way to explain the question she had been about to ask.

"What, dear? Did we see what?" her mother asked.

"Nothing. Nothing, Mama." Amy backed toward the door. "I better hurry up and get dressed."

"There's oatmeal on the back of the stove," Aunt Abigail called after her. "Your mother and I ate hours ago."

Amy dressed quickly, ate her breakfast, and plunged

into an enormously busy day. There was a washing to do, clothes to be folded away in the steamer trunk, and all the other possessions of the Polonskis to be wrapped and packed away in crates and boxes. But whether she was cranking the handle of the wringer, hanging out clothes on the backyard line, or wrapping dishes in old newspapers, Amy's mind kept returning to the same question. Several times during the day, she managed a few private minutes, and each time she hurried to the storeroom, but although she looked under and behind every box and trunk and piece of furniture, she did not find the Stone.

* * *

The next morning Amy sat with her face pressed against the train window and watched the Hills fade farther and farther away into a gray-blue haze. At the far end of the car three men, members of the train's crew, sat around a table playing cards and drinking coffee. Across from Amy, her parents were talking to a Mr. Randolph. Mr. Randolph was the only other passenger on the milk train that went through the town of Lambertville very early in the morning. Amy's parents and Mr. Randolph were talking about the inconvenience of having to ride on a train that stopped at practically every farm all the way across the valley, and about how nice it had been when, for a short while just before the Depression, a real passenger train had gone through Lambertville and the other foothill towns. Now and then Amy listened for a moment, particularly when her father talked about the train trestles that he had helped build all across the state. But most of the time she had other things on her mind. Most of the time, with her face pressed hard against the window, Amy looked back and thought about the past—the past few days, and other pasts, more distant and mysterious. There was so much that was mysterious, and so much to wonder about.

There was, for instance, the Stone. Some time between the moment when Amy had dropped it as she jumped up to run, and eight-thirty the next morning, the Stone had disappeared as completely as if it had dissolved into thin air. At times Amy thought perhaps it had. But at other times she thought that perhaps Aunt Abigail had found it and thrown it away. Knowing Aunt Abigail, it was hard to believe that she would have found a large rough rock on her storeroom floor and not even have mentioned it to the person most likely to be guilty of leaving it there. Knowing Aunt Abigail, it was almost easier to believe that a Stone could dissolve in thin air.

Wondering about the Stone was only a part of wondering about everything that had happened in the storeroom on Thursday night. Over and over again Amy wondered about what she had seen, picturing every detail as clearly and distinctly as she could.

It had all seemed so clear and close at the time, not vague and uncertain like the images in a dream. But looking back now, from the train—from Saturday morning, it was already beginning to fade. It was becoming hard to recall exactly how the faces had looked, and how terribly frightened she had felt when the man started toward her across the room.

Would it keep on fading? Amy wondered. Would a day come when she might not be sure anymore that the whole thing had not been just an ordinary dream?

But whatever it had been, it seemed to Amy that there was something about it that was very important, if she could just understand exactly what it meant. What did it mean about her grandfather and grandmother and the two little girls who had grown up to be her mother and aunt?

Going back into her farthest memories, Amy began to try to remember everything she had ever heard her mother and aunt say about their parents. There had been so much—so many stories. And yet nothing that explained the things that Amy had seen in the storeroom.

In her mother's stories, her grandfather had always been almost like God, strong and perfect—and Taylor Springs had been the most wonderful place in the world to grow up. But Aunt Abigail said different things. Aunt Abigail said that she had always hated Taylor Springs—and when she talked about their father, which was not very often, it was almost as if she were talking about a different person entirely.

It seemed strange to Amy now, thinking back, that

she had not wondered about the differences before. It was as if she had heard all the differences, and accepted them, without ever noticing that they did not seem to fit together. She would have to ask about a lot of things again, she decided, and listen more carefully to the answers. Even if she didn't hear anything new, she felt certain she could find out a lot by listening more carefully and noticing the way things were said.

She remembered, then, some things that had been said in just the last few days—things that she had not really listened to at the time because her mind had been so busy with other problems. She remembered how Aunt Abigail, who had always said she hated Taylor Springs, had said that she couldn't leave *now*—she had said *now*, but it had somehow sounded like *not ever*.

And Amy's mother, who had always made Taylor Springs sound like a kind of fairyland, had seemed really happy to be leaving. Of course, she might have been pretending to be happy because of Amy's father and the new job. But it hadn't sounded like pretending. It had sounded as if she herself, Helen Fairchild Polonski, was really glad to be getting away from Taylor Springs.

What did it mean? What did people mean by the things they said, and why did it seem so different sometimes from what was really happening? It was not that they were lying—that much was certain. Neither

Amy's mother nor Aunt Abigail would ever tell a lie on purpose. It could only be that they saw things differently.

"Something that one person would say is true, someone else would say wasn't." It was Jason who had said that.

And Amy had said, "Then one of them is lying," because she had always thought the *truth* was certain and final and for sure. But maybe Jason had been right about the truth. And after what had happened in the storeroom, it seemed as if he might have been right about time, too—about the way the past is a lot closer than most people think, and there can be times and places where it flows close enough to see and almost touch.

It seemed as if that part of what Jason had said might be true, but Amy still didn't know about the rest of it. There were a lot of things she still had to decide about. But that was all right, because there were probably some kinds of things—like Stone Hollow—that everyone had to decide about for himself. It was beginning to seem as if the world was full of things to find out about and decide for yourself.

The Hills had become a faint cloudy haze in the far distance when Amy sighed deeply and rubbed her nose where it felt flat and cold from the window glass. She got up, stretching, and crossed to the other side of the car. Through the windows on that side she could see the valley reaching on and on to the horizon.

And beyond the horizon was the coast range, and San Francisco, and the ocean, and on and on and on. Amy sighed again.

The train seemed to be moving so slowly—hardly as fast as a good runner could run. Amy began to imagine herself running, skimming over the ground beside the tracks. Watching the boulders and bushes drift by, she pictured herself bounding over them— flying over the earth with streaming hair and flashing feet.

For a long time she imagined herself running—up a steep incline and across a trestle bridge, leaping lightly from tie to tie, and then down a long slope to the valley floor.

"Amy," her father's voice said, and she turned to find him watching her. "What are you doing? You've been hunching your shoulders and twitching your arms back and forth."

Amy smiled sheepishly. "I was running," she said. "I was pretending I was running along by the tracks."

"Still running," her father grinned. He lowered his voice with exaggerated caution. "Don't let your mother hear about that."

To Amy's surprise her mother went along with the teasing. "What's this?" she said pretending dismay. "You haven't skinned another knee?"

"No, Mama," Amy laughed. "This time it was different."

The train clattered on. Amy rested her head against

the back of the seat and closed her eyes, still feeling the running in the muscles of her arms and legs, and seeing the land flying back—back into the distance.

Still running, she thought. Maybe she always would be. But it *had* been different this time, and not just that she had been imagining. That wasn't important. The important difference was that before she had never known why she was running. And this time she knew. This time she had just been hurrying to get to San Francisco—and whatever came after that.

LLOYD ALEXANDER

THE PRYDAIN CHRONICLES

These fantasy classics follow Assistant Pig-Keeper Taran and his companions through many magical adventures in their struggle against the evil Lord of Death. The five-book series is packed with action, humor, and gallantry that will keep readers of all ages coming back for more.

_____THE BOOK OF THREE $2.95 (40702-8)

_____THE BLACK CAULDRON $2.95 (40649-8)

_____THE CASTLE OF LLYR $3.25 (41125-4)

_____TARAN WANDERER $3.25 (48483-9)

_____THE HIGH KING............................. $3.25 (43574-9)

And ... revisit Prydain in the six enchanting short stories in:

_____THE FOUNDLING......................... $2.50 (42536-0)

YEARLING BOOKS